RITUAL OF PASSION,
TRIAL BY THE SWORD . . .

She wore bracelets on both arms, silver anklets and necklaces, garlands of flowers around head, neck, and waist—and nothing else. Her voice rose and fell in a long melodic song, and Falcon watched, spellbound by the mind-numbing rhythms of the music and the beauty of the woman. At the fine symmetry of her body, the taut white flesh, the rich throatiness of her voice, he found himself seized in the grip of a passion that was utterly primitive. So caught up was he in the woman's spell that he did not notice he was surrounded until the men were within arm's reach. . . .

THE BLACK POPE

⊘

Exciting Fiction From SIGNET

THE FALCON #2

THE BLACK POPE

by
Mark Ramsay

A SIGNET BOOK
NEW AMERICAN LIBRARY
TIMES MIRROR

For Al-Barran and the Society for Creative Anachronism

ONE

THE mountain stream roared from the mouth of the granite-walled gorge with the bellow of an angry dragon. The winter had been hard, with heavy snows, and the spring runoff was heavy, swelling the stream to many times its normal flow. On the bank, two mounted men stared gloomily into the stream, where a few jagged pilings revealed the former location of a wooden bridge.

"It must've washed out days ago." The speaker was a tall, lean man in the long-sleeved mailcoat of a knight. Just now, the coif of mail which would cover his head and face in battle hung down his back, revealing a deeply tanned face of hawklike planes and angles. His hair was jet-black except for a vivid white streak springing from the brow. From the bottom of the white blaze, a thin white line traced its way down his face and neck to disappear beneath the iron links of his hauberk.

"Shall we go downstream?" said the other man. "Maybe we'll come across another bridge." He was a few years younger than the other, and he wore a short, sleeveless jerkin of mail. Shaggy yellow locks hung from beneath his rounded steel cap.

"We've little choice," said the tall knight. "Leave a sign for the others."

The blond man-at-arms dismounted and poked about the ruins of the bridge until he found a short piece of board. This he fastened to one of the remaining piers. Apparently the bridge had been a popular campsite, and with the charred end of a stick he traced a crude but recognizable picture of a bird of prey with outstretched wings and an arrow pointing downstream. He stepped back to admire his artistry for a moment, then remounted. In silence, the two men rode, and behind them towered the magnificent peaks of the Alps in whose foothills they had been riding for days. The region was sparsely populated, with steep, thin-soiled fields little suited for farming. Most of the people were shepherds who lived a semi-nomadic existence, following their sheep and goats from pasture to pasture. Occasionally, a shepherd on a hillside would catch sight of the two horsemen, but when they sought to ask directions, the man would flee, leaving his flock and his dogs and heading for the cover of the nearest trees.

"What has the people here so frightened?" wondered the younger man.

"Who knows?" The other shrugged his massive shoulders. "It won't be the first land we've traveled through where armed men are an unwelcome sight."

At midday they came to the ruins of a village. The scene was one of utter devastation. Every house had been burned to the ground and the ruins were still smoking. There were few bodies about, mostly those of elderly people, but all had been hideously mutilated. Even cats and dogs had been killed. The only stone building in the village was a small church, which still stood, seemingly untouched.

"Is there war hereabouts?" asked the younger man.

"This is a little thorough, even for a war," said the other. "Maybe a blood feud with another village. It looks as if all the livestock have been driven off, along with all the able-bodied men and women. Let's look in the church. If the priest lived through it he can tell us what's happened here."

"What for?" asked the younger man. "Whatever happened is none of our affair."

"I like to know who's killing whom and why, in land I'm passing through." The tall man with the white blaze dismounted and walked up the four stone steps into the church, followed by the man-at-arms. At first they could see nothing in the dim interior, but the smell that assailed them was staggering. Slowly, their eyes adjusted to the dim light and they took in the full horror of the scene. The narrow, cramped interior was crammed with bodies of men, women, and children, their corpses so mutilated that age and sex were at best matters of guesswork. The altar was so soaked with blood that it was clear that most of the butchery had been performed there. The figure of Christ had been torn from the crucifix above the altar and replaced by the body of the village priest. His genitals had been cut off and stuffed in his mouth.

Hardened warriors that they were, the two men were struck dumb by the sight. Abruptly, the taller spun on his heel and strode from the church. The other followed. They mounted and rode from the destroyed village in silence. The younger was first to speak. "I think we should wait for the others," he said. "They can't be more than an hour or two behind." His master merely grunted. "It's not blood feud, and it's not war," the younger man went on. "So what is it? I've never seen anything like it."

"Don't talk like a fool, Wulf," said the other. "We've both seen worse, in Palestine and elsewhere. Acre was worse than that. So was the march through Hungary."

"It's different," the yellow-haired man maintained. "That's war between Christian and heathen. Besides, I wasn't in Hungary, though you've told me about it often enough."

"What's the difference?" said the tall man bitterly. "A synagogue full of Jews set afire or a church full of slaughtered Christians. The stink's about the same."

"But why here? This is a Christian country. Why the sacrilege and the desecration of the church? Christians kill each other readily, I'll admit, but why such butchery?"

"I intend to find out."

The sun was lowering in the west when they heard the first sounds. Above the roaring of the stream, they could hear the tramp of iron-shod hoofs and the clink of arms. Before them, the narrow road wound into the deep shade of a patch of forest, and it was from the woods that the sounds were coming. The knight drew the mail coif over his head and pulled its dangling veil across his mouth and nose, tying it at the temple. Now his face was completely sheathed in iron except for the pale, gray eyes. From the pommel of his saddle he took a tall, pointed helmet, splendidly forged from a single piece of iron, and strapped it on. Its thick nasal bar bisected the coif's vision slit. He drew on a pair of thick black leather gloves, densely studded on their backs with pointed iron studs. Next he took the long, triangular shield from behind his saddle and hung it by his neck strap across his back. It could be shifted to the front and his arm thrust through the arm straps in a moment. On the shield was painted a black bird of prey, clutching in its claws bolts of blue lightning. He checked to be sure that his sword was loose in its sheath and that the thong by which his ax was slung from his saddle pommel was loose and free of kinks. Satisfied with his preparations, he sat easily and awaited whatever might befall.

A file of horsemen emerged from the treeline. The

4

knight studied them closely, counting as they rode into view. There were seven. All were in mail. All were helmed. All bore identical black shields. Their helms and armor were likewise black. The helms were flat-topped and completely covered their faces, presenting only blank eye slits. Face-covering helms had been in use for several years, but they were still rare. The knight had never seen a whole party equipped with them. Most bizarre of all were the crests of the helms. All were adorned with horns, wings, talons, antlers, dragon spines, or other fantastic ornaments.

When they caught sight of the knight and his companion the horsemen spread out into a line abreast and walked slowly forward in ominous silence. They drew rein a few paces from the two.

"Who are you?" The voice rang hollowly from within the closed helmet.

"My name is Draco Falcon," the knight said. "Who are you?"

"Who we are is of no consequence. We have no names." The speaker wore a helm with curling ram's horns sprouting from its sides. "You are warriors and so we must make the offer. If you wish to live, you must join us. Renounce your king or other lord. Renounce your family and renounce God. Swear fealty to our master and all we have will be yours."

"There was a village back there"—the knight jerked a thumb over his shoulder—"but no longer. Was that your doing?"

"It was. Join us and you may enjoy sport like that every day. Join or die!"

"Don't mistake us for unarmed villagers, you murdering pig!" shouted Falcon. "Out of our way or you'll be puking blood into that iron bucket!" The seven laughed maniacally.

"Kill them!" said the man with the ram's horns.

At these words, the man-at-arms kicked a leg over his saddle and landed on the ground with a small iron shield in one hand and a short curved sword in the other. At the same instant, the knight shifted his shield before his body and snatched up his ax.

A man with bat's wings on his helm couched his lance and charged Falcon. The knight shoved the lance point to the right with the edge of his shield and stood on his stirrups. The ax came whistling down, its broad blade shearing through the iron helm and stopping at the man's collarbones. Falcon dug in his spurs and his horse leaped forward, dragging the ax free with a sickening squelch. Instead of swerving to engage the next man on one side or the other, Falcon simply charged his big destrier straight into the other horse, bowling it over to send the rider sprawling on the ground. His horse sprang over the other and then he was through the line, with Wulf running close behind. The unhorsed man scrambled to his feet, but Wulf, without breaking stride, thrust the point of his sword beneath the edge of the black helm and the man fell back, spraying blood.

Falcon wheeled his mount and faced the line of stunned horsemen. "How do you like this 'sport,' pigs?" he taunted. "A little more lively than butchering villagers, eh?" He charged the opposing line again, forcing his way between two of the riders. He blocked a sword slash from the left-hand man with his shield while ducking the sword of the other, then straightened and slammed a backhand blow of his ax into the right-hand rider's spine as he passed. Before the left-hand man could recover, Wulf was straddling the saddle behind him, one arm around the man's chest as he thrust his sword under the helm and into his neck.

"Spread out, you fools!" screamed the man with the ram's horns. The remaining three horsemen split up to give themselves more fighting room. Falcon felt a rap at his leg and looked down. Wulf was afoot again.

"I hear horsemen coming, Draco. It may be more of them. Let's ride out of here."

Falcon looked at him with rage-glazed eyes. "These swine have lived too long. I'll finish them or die myself!"

Wulf shrugged philosophically. "If you must. Take the one with the ram's horns first. He seems the most dangerous."

Falcon wheeled his mount and charged the black leader. The man with the ram's horns lowered his lance and charged in turn. The lance caught Falcon's shield dead center, slamming it back against his body and causing him to miss with the first blow of his ax. The two horses circled one another, kicking and biting. The black-armored man dropped his lance and drew sword. Falcon blocked a cut with his shield and replied with a chop that split the black shield and bit into his opponent's arm. The man howled and tried to pull free, but the ax was firmly wedged. Falcon backed his horse and hauled the other man out of his saddle. As the black horseman crashed to the ground, Falcon released the ax and drew his sword. Its blade was long, broad, and curved, wider at the tip than at the hilt. With a backhanded slash, he hewed at the neck below the edge of the black helmet. Helmet and head leaped free and the body stood for a moment as if searching for its missing parts before crashing to the ground.

"Here they come!" shouted Wulf. Falcon looked up to see the two remaining horsemen charging down on him, one from each side. If he engaged one, the other was sure to skewer him. Nevertheless, he wheeled to charge one of them. There was a faint whispering in the air, then both black riders were tumbling from their saddles, each with a yard-long shaft protruding from his mail.

Two men rode up to Falcon and Wulf. They wore no

armor, but each carried a six-foot bow. Behind them rode another twoscore horsemen. All the others were armored, armed to the teeth, and splendidly mounted.

"Gower, Rhys," Falcon said. "I thank you. They almost had me." Two more men rode up. One was a burly man with a hideously scarred face. The other was old and gray-bearded and one-eyed, with a great potbelly.

"I knew we shouldn't have let you ride ahead," said the scarred man. "You always get into trouble and have to be rescued. You've been busy, I see." He surveyed the corpses that littered the ground. He spoke with a marvelously barbarous Irish accent.

"Be these the buggers that did for that village back there?" the old man asked.

"So they said," Falcon replied. "But why, I don't know. They talked like madmen."

"Never seen anything like these turd-suckers," the old man mused. "Don't care to see any more of 'em, neither. I've been to the wars more than twoscore years, here and in Outremer, but that village back there'd make a maggot in a leper's sores puke." The old man, called Rupert Foul-Mouth for obvious reasons, was Falcon's master siege engineer.

"All armored alike, except for the horns and such," mused the scarred man, an Irishman named Donal MacFergus. "What do you make of them, my lord?"

"They're a mystery to me," Falcon said. Some of his men had dismounted and were efficiently stripping the bodies of weapons and armor and clothes while others rounded up the horses. Falcon half expected them to be horned and tusked and hairy beneath the ominous black armor, but they were men like any others.

"Let's ride down out of these damned hills and find a way across this river," Falcon said. They rode away from the bloody field, leaving the seven naked bodies for whatever scavengers wanted them.

The town was not very large, but at least its people did not run away at the sight of a band of armed men. It was walled and had a spacious inn, but best of all it had a fine stone bridge. A Provençal dialect was spoken here, and the town seemed to gain its prosperity from the presence of the old stone bridge, the only reliable river crossing for many leagues. Falcon saw to the picketing of the beasts in the town common and then went with most of his men to the inn.

Many heads turned as they passed into the low-beamed common room, where welcome smells of food, wine, and ale met their nostrils. The men sat at the long benches and began calling for food and drink. Wulf helped his master divest himself of the long mail hauberk, pulling the heavy garment off as Falcon bent forward, turning the coat inside out as it rolled over his head and down his arms. Wulf carefully rolled the precious armor up, then stowed it in its oiled-leather bag. He then yanked his own mail jerkin off and dropped it unceremoniously into the straw at his feet.

The serving staff brought bread and cheeses, then sausages and meats of many kinds, all with plentiful wine and ale. The innkeeper was inquisitive.

"Are you gentlemen just returned from Outremer?" he asked, between courses. Outremer meant "oversea," and it was the common name for the incredible kingdoms and countries the Crusaders had established from Asia Minor to Egypt.

"Some of us have been there, but not recently," Falcon said. "We're free warriors, and we fight for whoever will pay us."

"Free soldiers?" this from a man in the rich furs of a merchant, who sat across the table from Falcon. "And you hire out as a group? That I've never heard of before."

"It's been done for years in Palestine," Falcon replied.

"These men have sworn their fealty to me, and I find employment for us all. Just now we want to get across this accursed river. There's a Savoyard noble a few leagues north who wants to hire us for the siege he's laying to a kinsman's castle. We're late as it is."

"A landless lord," muttered the merchant. "How original."

Comfortably stuffed, Falcon called for one of his men to bring him one of the bags that had been propped against a wall of the common room. "Gentlemen," he addressed the merchant and innkeeper, "does this mean anything to you?" He reached into the bag and pulled out the ram's-horn helm, plunking it onto the middle of the table.

The effect could not have been greater had a demon materialized on the spot. The innkeeper jumped back a yard or two, making signs against the evil eye, and the merchant turned deathly pale. All over the room, men jumped to their feet, overturning benches and spilling pitchers of wine and ale. A priest who had been eating at a far corner of the room came running over and stared with horror at the helmet, clutching his crucifix. "Where did you get this?" demanded the priest.

"From its wearer," said Falcon, mystified. "I took his head, too, but I had no use for that. There were six others and we killed them all, but there must be many more of them. They took a village two days' ride north of here and killed everyone in it. They all wore gear like this. What does it mean?"

"Bless you, my lord," the priest said. "Even if you had never gone on Crusade, killing these demons would have ensured your salvation. These monsters are the devil-worshiping followers of the heretic archbishop!"

"They've been ravaging the mountains northeast of here for months," the merchant said. "They kill all they encounter, men, women, children, taking only portable goods and livestock back to their mountain stronghold. A few have escaped, or observed them without being seen. It was from them that we learned of their black shields and armor, and the strange helms."

"They are not human," said the priest. "They are monsters and demons, shape-changers with the powers of Satan behind them."

"They were just men in outlandish gear who talked like moonstruck fools," Falcon said. "They were no harder to kill than others I've encountered."

"That is good to hear, sir," said the innkeeper. "The village you spoke of, that must be Rapides. What did you find there?"

Falcon described the carnage at the village and the obscene crucifixion in the church.

"I will go to the baron myself," said the priest. "He is back from the Holy Land now and he must take action! That whole region has reeked of paganism and heresy for generations. I will demand that he mount a Crusade to clean those mountain valleys out for good!" At this there were dark looks and mutterings from the crowd assembled in the room. Neither the church nor its Crusades were very popular in the Provençal-speaking regions.

When most of the others lay snoring in the straw, Falcon and the merchant sat up by candlelight, drinking wine and talking. The merchant made several trips each year, and Falcon wanted to know what was occurring in the north and west. He heard about Richard of England's ravagings in the north. For personal reasons, Falcon harbored a violent hatred of Richard and he made no secret of it.

"So you don't share the general admiration of the chivalrous Lion-Heart?" the merchant asked.

"Richard's a bloodthirsty maniac. What he did at Acre was nothing but useless cruelty. If he's the best chivalry has to offer, then I want no part of it." Falcon stared morosely into his winecup.

"You refer to the slaughter of the prisoners. We've heard of that. So you were at the great siege, sir?"

"I was." Falcon did not tell the merchant that he had not been outside the city with the Crusading army but inside, with the Saracens.

The merchant seemed to weigh his next words carefully, but when they came they seemed to be apropos of nothing. "The winter was severe. Many of the young lambs died."

Frowning, Falcon wondered what the man was getting at. The merchant was toying idly with the hilt of his dagger, and Falcon saw that the brass pommel of the dagger was engraved with the figure of a lamb. Then he remembered. It had been the hermit in the woods last year, the one who had nursed him through his recurring fever. The man had spoken of something called the Order of Light, a band of church and lay people who were striving to bring about an end to the brutality of the times. They recognized one another through the sign of the lamb, and by speaking of "lambs and winter." From the pouch at his belt, Falcon withdrew the leaden seal from his belt and held it dangling by its thong so that the merchant could see the lamb inscribed upon it.

"I thought you might be one of us," the man said, leaning forward conspiratorially.

"Not one of you," Falcon corrected, "but I was once helped by one of your order. He gave me this and told me of your password. He had no need of my aid, but I'm a man who pays his debts."

"Then stay in this district. You heard that priest. He's going to get the local baron to mount a Crusade against the heretics."

"And why not?" Falcon said. "It sounds like a fine idea to me."

"Thousands of innocent people will be slaughtered to wipe out a few score black-armored madmen. The people of those mountain valleys are harmless folk, for the most part, but they are primitive and hold to the old ways, the ancient religions. You know that to Crusaders all heretics seem alike. The bloodshed will be terrible and needless. If you and your men were to take care of the archbishop and his butchers, then there would be no need for a Crusade."

Falcon pondered this awhile. "I'm sorry," he said at length. "My first obligation is to my men, and I've contracted for them to take service with this Savoyard. Without gainful employment we all starve. I must look to their welfare first."

"That is sad news," said the merchant, downcast. "Now we must all suffer, for the Crusade will be worse than the ravages of de Beaumont's men."

Suddenly, Draco Falcon was a man transformed. He reached across the table and grasped a handful of the merchant's robe. He dragged the man bodily across the table and held the merchant's face within inches of his own. "Did you say de Beaumont?"

"Why, yes," spluttered the merchant. "That's the name of their leader, Archbishop de Beaumont." The merchant was frightened at the sudden change in his companion. Falcon released his hold and the merchant sat heavily back on his bench.

"Tell me more," Falcon said.

"Why, there's little more to tell. The man is said to be a Fleming. He is supposed to have accompanied the Crusade, only to come back horribly changed. He was excommunicated for heresy and came into this district with his band of killers a few months ago, and set up in an ancient abbey in the mountains, near a village called Goatsfoot, where they practice their barbarous rites. Does the name mean something to you?"

13

Falcon said nothing for a long time. Then he took a long swallow of his wine and smiled benignly. "Archbishop de Beaumont," he said. "I may be able to do you a service after all."

Early the next morning, the bulk of Falcon's band crossed the bridge to join their Savoyard noble, but Falcon, Wulf, and a few others headed back up the river valley, toward the village called Goatsfoot.

TWO

THE mouth of the gorge they had passed some days before was still nearly filled by the turbulent stream. Falcon and the others peered into its depths, but the heavy mist raised by the stream's violent passage obscured vision past a score of paces. Just above the waterline, a narrow, rocky path snaked along the base of a flanking cliff, seemingly hand-hewn in some past age.

"Is that the only way we can take?" asked Wulf, dismayed.

"According to those villagers, it is," Falcon replied. In coming back through the destroyed village, they had found a party of people from a neighboring hamlet who had come to bury the dead. They had tried to flee at the approach of the armed men, but Falcon's men had rounded up a few and convinced them of their benign intent. When asked about Goatsfoot they had refused to answer at first, making ritual gestures and clutching crucifixes and lucky charms.

At last one of the villagers had summoned the courage to speak. He was typical of the hill people of the area— tall, fair-haired, ruddy of complexion. The people of these hills were so inbred that any two could have been taken for siblings. The man had said that the village and others like it beyond the gorge were accursed, that their people were witches and shape-changers and they were only seen once or twice each year when they came down from their mountains to barter for goods they could not produce for themselves. Little more was known about them, or else the villagers would tell no more.

"Do you think it's true, my lord?" Wulf asked, his eyes striving vainly to pierce the dimness of the gorge. "About the people being witches, I mean?"

"Have you ever been in a village where the people *didn't* say that the next village down the road or across the river or up in the hills was full of witches and were-wolves?" Falcon glared into the gorge. He was no more anxious than Wulf to enter its mysterious depths, and he knew that he was just stalling here, talking nonsense with Wulf. "You say it yourself about those Scots across your borders."

"But there *are* witches up there!" Wulf protested.

"Enough of this," Falcon said. "Get ready to take the trail." Falcon and the others dismounted to strip off their armor, except for the two Welshmen, who never wore it. A man in mail who fell into deep water would sink like a stone. Not that he would have much of a chance in this torrent, but any chance was better than none.

Besides Falcon, Wulf, and the Welshmen, the band included Donal MacFergus, the hideously scarred Irishman; and Simon, the ex-monk who had found his true vocation in soldiering. The rest of Falcon's little army had gone on to their appointment under Falcon's second-in-command, Sir Ruy Ortiz, a Spanish knight who was master of horse and standard-bearer of the band.

Falcon rode in the lead, his great curved sword drawn. All the others except the Welshmen were likewise prepared for instant combat, as they had no idea what to expect on the other side of the gorge. Donal bore a wide-bladed Irish ax, and Simon a morningstar—a spiky iron ball attached to a wooden handle by a two-foot chain. Wulf had his short falchion and buckler at the ready. The Welshmen rode in the rear, their great yew bows cased and their bowstrings coiled under their caps, since the dampness of the roiling mist would quickly render them useless.

The cramped narrowness of the gorge depressed the men's spirits, and the roar of the stream made conversation impossible. The horses could proceed only at the slowest walk, and the riders had to keep their attention firmly on the narrow, slippery stone path. Falcon found himself marveling at the path, which must have been carved from the solid granite with untold labor. At the relatively unworn edges of the path the chisel marks were still discernible. Such a thing was surely beyond the powers of the primitive hill people. Falcon amused himself by trying to calculate how many iron chisels must have been worn out in making this path, and his mind reeled at the thought. Iron was a rare and precious metal, only a little less valuable than silver and gold. Few kings of this age could afford such a lavish expenditure of iron to make a path linking mountain villages.

The path climbed gradually along the face of the cliff until the men were riding high above the stream. Abruptly, they emerged from the mist. The sky was overcast, but after the dank dimness of the gorge the day seemed bright and cheerful. Shortly after emerging from the mist, they came to the end of the path. At the mouth of the gorge, the land widened out into a broad meadow. Where the path ended, there was a tall stone pillar, crudely carved from the local rock and erected to some unknown purpose in ages past. As the men redonned their war gear, they studied the monolith with an interest that contained an element of superstitious awe.

"There was a standing stone like that outside my village in England," Wulf said. "The people there said it was put up by fairies."

"They're all over Ireland," Donal observed, wiping the drops of condensation from his ax.

"There are whole fields of them in Brittany, I've heard," said Simon.

"Whoever made them has been dead a long time," Falcon said. "I'm more interested in the men with the black shields and their leaders. Mount and let's ride."

The highland valley was stark and bare, mostly rock and steep meadows. High above them, they could see twin peaks, still snow-covered, with a low pass between them.

They saw no people, but evidence of habitation was all about, and most of it of a disquieting nature. They passed a row of stakes, each surmounted by the skull of some animal. There were more standing stones, some large and others small, some arranged in circles and others in gate-like form, with two upright stones and a third laid across them like a lintel. The road from the gorge was so seldom-used that it could scarcely be seen, but here and there they found the marks of iron-shod horses, undoubtedly those of the black warriors. These recent marks branched off onto a sidetrack that led upward toward the pass.

"Shall we follow them?" Wulf asked.

"Not until we have a better idea of what we might find," Falcon answered. "Let's locate that village first and see if we can't pry some answers from the inhabitants."

The trail led them to a shallow, tree-filled depression covering several acres, a dense forestation uncommon so high up. The sun was almost down and the path was dark within the trees, but they could make out garlands of flowers hanging from the low branches, and certain trees had odd-looking strings of charms girdling their trunks. Falcon held up his hand and halted the column.

"What is it?" Wulf asked. Falcon seemed to be listening intently.

"Don't you hear it?" Falcon said. They strained their ears, then the sounds separated themselves from the ordinary noises of a forest; rhythmic, staccato beats and what might have been voices chanting. In the eerie confines of the darkling forest it was a hackle-raising sound, and many of the men felt a profound dread.

"It must be those black devils practicing their rites," Donal said.

"I don't think so," Falcon replied. "They rode off uphill. Our best course is to make camp and wait until daylight, but I want to see what is going on up ahead." He turned to the two Welshmen. "Gower, Rhys, you two hold the horses. The rest of us are going to proceed on foot." Reluctantly, the others dismounted.

Falcon led the way. Their soft boots made little sound on the trail, and only the faint rustle of their mail was alien to the forest. Wulf, Donal, and Simon bore shields, and these they carried well away from their bodies and weapons to avoid a betraying clatter.

Slowly, the dimness of the forest was relieved by a dull, ruddy glare. Their steps slowed as they came to a clearing from which the light emanated. Screening themselves behind trees and brush, they approached the edge of the clearing. The sounds were distinct now; a rattle of percussion, made by tiny drums beaten by sticks, a high, nerve-rending wail of flutes, the sound of chants endlessly repeated.

From behind a tree, Falcon studied the scene in the clearing. A large bonfire had been built, near the base of a huge standing stone. Around fire and stone, people danced. There were at least a hundred of them, some in the skins of animals, some in clothes of homespun, others naked. To one side a small band produced the wild music on crude instruments and the bare feet of the dancers stamped in time to the music. The glare of the fire cast wild shadows on the monolith and against the surrounding forest wall.

A man leaped between the fire and the stone. He was dressed from head to foot in stag skins, and on his head he wore the huge antlers of the male of the species. Even in the firelight, Falcon could tell that the antlers were very ancient. The man held a rattle in one hand, which he clattered incessantly. In the other, he held a bunch of mistletoe. A girl of about ten, naked except for a garland of flowers around her head, held up a bowl. The stag-man dipped the mistletoe into the bowl and used it to sprinkle a liquid onto the dancers as they passed, all the while crying out a chant in some language that Falcon could not recognize.

The stag-man and the little girl left, and their place was taken by a woman. She wore bracelets on both arms, and silver anklets and necklaces, garlands of flowers around head, neck, and waist, and nothing else.

Her height was difficult to judge from Falcon's distance, but her body was full and statuesque, with large breasts, rounded hips, and sturdy thighs. Her hair was midnight black and she moved with a fine, animal grace. She raised her arms and called out in the same strange language. Her voice rose and fell in a long, melodic song, and the people continued to dance in their circle, clapping and stamping in time to the woman's voice.

Falcon was spellbound by the primeval scene, the mind-numbing rhythms of the music, and the beauty of the woman. At the fine symmetry of her body, the taut, white flesh, the rich throatiness of her voice, he found himself seized in the grip of a passion which was utterly primitive in its generalized lust. Somehow, he knew that this was what the ritual was all about.

He and the others were so enthralled by the scene that

they did not notice they were surrounded until the men were within arm's reach.

Falcon was first to break from his trance. He whirled, snatching out his curved sword. Belatedly, the others did likewise. There were at least thirty men in the group which surrounded them. They were smaller and darker than the people of the lower hills. None seemed to be armed, and their attitude was more watchful than threatening. Among them was the stag-man. Simon started whirling the ball of his morningstar.

"Stop," Falcon said, levelly. "We've no quarrel with these people. Don't fight unless attacked." He faced the stag-man. "We mean no harm." He hoped that the man knew the dialect of the lowlands, a corrupt form of Provençal.

"Why do you spy upon our festival?" The voice from inside the stag mask was deep and mellow, its accent peculiar.

"We were following the trail, looking for a town called Goatsfoot," Falcon said. "We heard the sounds and came to investigate. We did not intend to profane your rites."

"Not many come this way from below," the stag-man said. "What is your business?"

"We've come to investigate the men in black who have been ravaging in the low country. Their depredations put you all in great danger."

The stag-man seemed to consider for a moment. "You must come talk to the Old Woman. First take off your iron."

With poor grace but little choice, the men divested themselves of weapons and armor. Even spurs and buckles had to be left behind, if they were of iron. Before they were permitted within the clearing, the antlered man sprinkled them with his mistletoe aspergillum. Then they were led into the firelight.

The dancing and music faltered and stopped as the

band were led to the fire. All eyes were on them. Falcon looked about for some elderly matriarch who must interview them. The lovely, black-haired woman walked around the fire and strode up to Falcon, magnificently unself-conscious in her nudity. The stag-man faced her.

"Old Woman," he said, "this one is their leader, and he says they mean no harm." She looked at Falcon, then stepped so close that he could feel the animal heat of her body. She touched his brow, traced the fine white line down his face to his neck.

"You are marked," she said. Her voice was husky almost to the point of hoarseness. "Lightning did this."

"It did," Falcon said.

"You must have great magic to have lived. We will talk later. You have been purified, so you may stay for the rest of the rite." She turned and walked back to the standing stone and resumed her chant. Falcon and the others were shown a place to sit next to the musicians. The two Welshmen were led in, looking shamefaced.

"We never saw them," Rhys said. "We were alone, then they were all around us."

"It's their country," Falcon said. "We might as well have tried to spy on Bedouin in the desert." The Welsh brothers sat down, and children brought bowls of ale and platters of food to the uninvited guests. This early in the year, the fare was mostly bread and cheese, but Falcon's men felt no hardship in this. The peasants of Europe ate little else in any case. The real feasts were held in the fall, after the harvests were in and when the animals that could not be fed through the winter were slaughtered.

Falcon tore into a loaf of black bread made from coarsely ground wheat, bristling with bran and bits of unseparated chaff. The cheese was made from goat's milk, strong and pungent. Falcon set his strong, white teeth into it with gusto. He had lived on far rougher food, and all food was precious. The ale was fine, strong and heady, and a good deal of it was necessary to wash down the dry food.

"What are they doing, my lord?" asked one of the Welshmen. A goat, decorated and beribboned, had been led to the tall stone. The stag-man cut its throat with a flint knife, and the carcass was cast onto the fire after the blood had drained into a stone trough. More animals stood in a forlorn line, awaiting their turn. Falcon saw an ox, a pony, a sheep, a pig, and several fowl. Around the fire, a man cavorted, dressed in the outsized feathers and comb of a cock.

"They're buying next year's prosperity," Falcon said. "Buying it with last year's blood." He peered into the dimness at the end of the line of beasts, afraid of what he might see. What would he do if there was a man there, or a woman or a child? Would he dare interfere and risk the lives of his men? What was this village to him?

"There were books in the monastery," Simon said, "that told of the old Romans and the Greeks. They had ceremonies like this." The ex-monk was proud of his learning. He could read Latin and knew how to add and subtract.

"You know," said Gower ap Gwynneth, his voice low and conspiratorial, "we used to do something like this in Wales, but we had to keep the priest—" His brother nudged him hard in the ribs and he fell silent.

Finally, the last of the animals was on the fire and the knife put back in its decorated skin bag, to Falcon's unutterable relief. The black-haired woman put on a doe's mask and began to dance with the stag-man. The dance ended with a mock copulation, the stag-man writhing over the woman's arched back and bellowing in an uncanny imitation of a rutting stag. Couples were wandering away from the fire, hand in hand, to lie at the edge of the trees. None went out of the clearing, and though the light was

23

dim so far from the fire, Falcon could see that there was nothing of the pantomime in what they were doing.

"It makes sense," Wulf said, grinning. "They've prayed for fertility, they've paid for it, now they're making sure their gods know exactly what it is they want."

"Do you think they'd mind if we joined in on this part?" said Donal, licking his jaggedly scarred lips as his eyes followed a plump young matron who had not found a partner for the proceedings at the edge of the clearing.

"Drink your ale and keep quiet," Falcon said. "I've been in places where we'd all have been castrated and hung over a slow fire for intruding on something like this. It goes on more than you'd think, in the remote places, even in Christendom."

As people came back from the edge of the clearing, they dipped blood from the trough into bowls. With their bowls, they disappeared into the night. The music ended, and the children, who were mostly asleep, were carried away by adults. The bonfire was burning low when the black-haired woman came to Falcon, wearing now a gown of heavy wool.

"Come with us to the village," she said. Falcon dismissed his men to gather up their arms and bring the horses. At the head of the band of villagers, Falcon walked beside the woman, their way flickeringly lit by the torches some of the people carried. She was shorter than Falcon had thought, and barely reached his chest, but she moved with the self-assured forthrightness of a queen.

"What do they do with the blood?" Falcon asked.

"They sprinkle it on their houses, on their fields and flocks. It will bring luck and plenty for the year." She looked up at him, studying his commanding height and lionlike bearing. "What am I to call you, lowlander?"

"I am Draco Falcon, captain of free soldiers." He gazed down at her. "And you?"

"My name is Lilitha. I am Old Woman of Goatsfoot. I

24

had the title from my mother, and her mother, and all my ancestresses back to the time of the gods. We see few lowlanders here, and there is no war. Why do you warriors come here?"

"There is liable to be war soon," Falcon said.

"Because of the black riders in iron?"

"Yes. They've been raiding in the lowlands, slaughtering entire villages with great cruelty."

"And what are these lowlanders to us?" the woman said. "For all the generations of my village they have been of no help to us. There are no marriage bonds or ties of kinship between us. They have never suffered over our woes, so why should we over theirs?"

"You have no choice," Draco replied. "The men in black have made a nuisance of themselves and the lowlanders are preparing a Crusade against them. You know what a Crusade is, don't you?"

"I've heard. Even up here, we get news of the world outside, from time to time. And if they come and clean out the black riders, will they leave us in peace?"

"I know Crusaders, Lilitha," Falcon said. "They make no distinction between one type of unbeliever and another. Once they start killing, there's no stopping them." The woman stayed silent in deep thought until they came to the village. In the darkness, all Falcon could make out was that it seemed small, and smelled about the same as any other village.

"Your men will be given places to sleep," Lilitha said. "Come with me." She led him to a house, seemingly no different from others in the village. It was built of small logs laid horizontally and chinked with clay, and it had a steeply pitched roof to shed the heavy winter snows. Inside it was pitch black until the woman built up a fire from the coals that glowed in the stone fireplace in the center of the dirt floor.

When there was sufficient light, Falcon could see that

the small, single room was spare but very clean, with bunches of herbs and dried vegetables hanging from the low rafters. The woman poked at the fire until she was satisfied with it, then she motioned to Falcon to sit on a pile of skins across the fire from her. The light of the fire, coming from below, cast deep shadows around her eyes and gave her a forbidding, almost sinister look.

"Have you had enough to eat?" she asked.

"Plenty," Falcon said. She took two bowls to a large stone crock that stood in a corner and dipped them in. One she handed to Falcon, now brimming with ale. He took a drink. It was as good as that at the ceremony, and flavored with some bitter herb.

"Tell me, warrior," the woman said at length, "why you have come here. Our people are nothing to you. Is there something between you and the black riders?"

"There is," Falcon admitted. "Their leader is a man I knew many years ago. He is a renegade archbishop who threw in with the Saracens. He is also one of four who betrayed, tortured, and murdered my father."

"So it is revenge you want, not to help us."

"If I can accomplish the one, the other will follow naturally." He took another long drink of the ale. "What I don't understand is why they have left you alone when they've acted so savagely down below."

"They have come to the village a few times, and taken men to work on the old Christian place where they live. The men rebuilt the old walls where they had fallen down. The riders told them what to do, but said nothing else."

"What happened to the Christians who once had that place?" Falcon asked.

"That was in my grandmother's day. The Christian holy men came up here praying and converting and saying that our ways are wrong. They said that we should not sacrifice blood because their god's son had been sacri-

26

ficed and no more blood was needed. They converted many, at first."

"What happened?"

"The crops failed, and the beasts bore few young and the people went hungry. So the Christians were driven out and we went back to our old ways."

"Have you seen the leader of the black riders?" Falcon asked.

"Never. Some have seen him, and they say he is a big, fat man in black robes, but he has never been to this village."

Falcon nodded. That sounded like de Beaumont, all right. The Flemish prelate had a deceptively soft, jolly, rubicund appearance, but the rolls of fat sheathed an iron frame, and the archbishop rode into battle at the head of his men wearing armor beneath his robes, brandishing a huge wooden club. He used the club because, having taken holy orders, he was forbidden to "smite with the edge of the sword."

"Tomorrow," Falcon said, "I would like to see where they have set up. Will you give me a guide?"

The woman thought a minute. "Yes, I will give you a man to take you there. There is a place where you may get close without being seen. But I cannot let you go against the black riders until I have talked about it with the other villages. They have done us no harm yet, and what they do down below is no concern of ours."

"Don't take too long at it, Lilitha," Falcon cautioned. He yawned mightily. He was sleepier than even his long day's exertions might have justified. He wondered if the bitter herb in the ale might be some sort of soporific. The powerful lust he'd felt for Lilitha at the ceremony had dissipated. She was a lovely and desirable woman, but that was all. He was mystified at the powerful passion that she had been able to generate.

She gave him more skins to sleep on, and thick woolen

blankets, then watched him as he sank into a deep sleep. Soon he was muttering restlessly, his hands clenched as if he were gripping something, and moving slightly in a slow rhythm in time to his breathing. She wondered what he was holding in his sleep. She had never seen an ocean, nor any other body of water larger than a small mountain lake, and she had no way of knowing how a man's hands looked when they were gripping a thirty-foot sweep oar.

THREE

DRACO de Montfalcon was twenty-one years old, and for two of those years he had been chained to the oar bench of a Turkish galley. Rowing a galley was inhumanly brutal labor and only men of extraordinary strength and stamina could survive two years of it, but Draco de Montfalcon was such a man. Another such was his benchmate, Wulf, the yellow-haired Saxon who had been his horseboy in happier days. The battle of Hattin had ended that. As he rowed, the beating of the time-keeper's drum turned into a litany of four names, which reeled endlessly through his mind, as they had for the last two years: Edgehill, FitzRoy, Valdemar, de Beaumont, over and over again.

The four had betrayed his father and they had betrayed the Crusader army into near annihilation at Hattin, but it was Valdemar who had captured Draco and Wulf and sold them onto this galley. The galley, named *Fatima,* was a lean, snakelike ship, a raider and plunderer, preying with fine impartiality on Christian and Moslem alike. Christian prisoners might be held for ransom, but Moslems were invariably sent to feed the fish, because the

29

ship's master, Rustam the Magnanimous, was concerned for his reputation. He had earned his name by contributing generously to mosques and holy men ashore, but only in the ports where he had to put in to sell his goods and take on supplies.

Falcon stared with hating, salt-reddened eyes at the man who paced down the catwalk between the oar pits; Abu, the overseer. He was a grossly fat man with a shaven head and a big black mustache that drooped to his chest. He was barefoot and wore only a loincloth and wide leather bracelets. Except in battle, he never bore a sword or dagger that some galley slave might snatch from him for purposes of murder or suicide. In his hand he held coiled a supple black whip of plaited rhinoceros hide. Abu's artistry with the whip was legendary among the Saracen fleets, for he had been expelled from a dozen galleys for his excessive cruelty. Besides his enormous love for blood and pain, Abu was fond of hashish and handsome young men. In their early days on the ship, Wulf and Falcon had been used for his perverted lusts, until younger, prettier boys were brought aboard. When he was not brooding his vengeance on his father's betrayers, Draco found time to plot ingenious ways to kill Abu.

"A sail!" The shout from the masthead lookout sent Abu and Rustam scampering into the rigging, shading their eyes as they strove to make out the prospective victim.

"A merchantman," Abu said.

"Probably out of Alexandria," Rustam commented excitedly. Alexandrine ships were often among the richest. "Prepare for action." Abu strode down the catwalk, popping his whip. The filthy, bearded, naked men at the oars prepared themselves for the terrible ordeal which might follow. Should the victim prove too strong, should a naval vessel appear on the scene, then they would have to flee. The rowers would have to row standing, one foot braced against the bench in front, bending to the angle and drawing back on each stroke until the rowers were stretched back almost horizontally across their benches, the oar butts touching their beards. This work could go on for hours, and after a long flight it was not uncommon to have five or six rowers dead from exhaustion.

Slaves came along the catwalk with buckets of sour wine in which poppy gum had been dissolved, giving each man a dipperful holding about a pint of the sustaining liquid. Falcon drank his drugged wine, feeling its faint numbness leaching the aches from his muscles and the sting of his most recent lashing from his back. His bench was padded with sheepskin. This was not for the comfort of the rowers but a dire necessity. The constant rubbing of the wooden bench could abrade buttocks through to the bone. Even with the sheepskins, a rower's thighs and buttocks were usually covered with sores or, if he was lucky, padded with thick callus.

The timekeeper's drum started again. There was no rush yet. The prey was a fat merchantman, far too slow to escape. The merchantman spread all sail, but its wallowing progress was as nothing to *Fatima's* predatory swoop. The galley drew inexorably closer, came up on the merchantman's stern.

"In oars!" Rustam cried. The rowers pulled the oars in as *Fatima* slid alongside the other ship and men in the bows cast grapples aboard the prey. Armed men prepared to board. Abu was at their head, a dagger through his loincloth and a short curved sword in his fist.

Suddenly, more grapples arched out from the merchantman, sinking into gunwales, tangling in the rigging, tying the two ships inextricably together. A horde of armed men burst through false decking on the merchantman and began striving to board *Fatima*.

"A trap!" Rustam shouted. "Cut loose! Cut loose!" Men chopped and sawed at the grapple lines with sword and ax as a storm of arrows and javelins poured aboard. The rowers watched disinterestedly. Whoever won, it would only be a change of masters. Falcon, though, studied the action with keen interest. Any change could be turned to good account. Also, he was concerned that Abu might be killed and Falcon cheated of his revenge.

In the stern of the "merchantman," Falcon saw a tall, gray-bearded man in a green turban directing the action. Falcon knew the green turban to be the sign of a descendant of the Prophet. Then he had to duck as another hail of missiles came aboard. Many of the rowers, unprotected, were killed or wounded. Falcon tugged in frustration at the chain that bound his ankle to the bench. If the ship sank, he would drown along with the other slaves. Worse would happen if *Fatima* was set afire.

"Get down, Norman!" It was the man who pulled the oar behind Falcon. Draco hunched as a jagged rock whistled through the space where his head had been. He twisted around. "Thanks, Irishman." The other man grinned. It was not a pretty sight. The Irishman had been captured from a Christian ship six months before. He was so powerful that he had at once been set to the oar, and so scarred that even Abu had never shown any interest in sodomizing him. For that, at least, Falcon envied him. The Irishman's mouth was twisted permanently half open from a sword or ax blow, and a horizontal slash had halved his nose and taken a piece out of one of his eyelids. Abu had once carved an ear from the man for snapping an oar by pulling on it too hard. The Irishman had laughed. His name was Donal something or other.

A knot of struggling men fell into the oar pit. The pirate catchers from the other ship had forced a boarding party onto *Fatima*. An ax fell at Falcon's feet, a tool for cutting rigging and boarding lines rather than a weapon. Its head was thick and heavy, without the fine balance of an ax designed for fighting. Falcon snatched it up. He eyed the chain at his ankle. It would be a difficult blow, striking almost straight down. Wulf, in front of him, was looking back. "Do it before they see you!" the Saxon pleaded.

"Give it to me!" the Irishman said. "Nobody can use an ax like me. I'll cut you loose first, then you can free me." Falcon thought for less than a second, then he slapped the haft of the ax into Donal's horny palm. The Irishman leaned forward and swung hard, a wide swing pivoting at the shoulder and much more powerful than any Falcon could have struck at his own chain. The link parted and Draco was free. He took the ax and with a mighty swing cut Wulf's chain. The ax was badly notched by now, and Falcon needed three blows to sever Donal's chain. He tossed the ax to Donal and picked up his oar. He raised the thirty-foot hardwood sweep over his head and brought it down hard on the gunwale. The oar broke and Falcon was left with a five-foot club.

A swing of the massive club cleared three of Rustam's pirates from the catwalk, and Falcon leaped up onto the wooden deck. He began methodically clearing the catwalk, taking out one or more pirates at every blow. Wulf and Donal scrambled up behind him. The arrows and javelins and rocks had stopped flying where men from the other ship had swarmed on *Fatima's* deck.

"Abu!" Falcon shouted. "I'm coming for you!" Wulf looked at his friend and former master. Draco was going into one of his berserker rages, the rages he had suffered periodically ever since he was struck by the lightning on the voyage to the Holy Land. Abu had loved to tease and goad Draco into that rage while protected by Draco's chains. Now Abu was going to pay.

The pirates went down like grain before the scythe, as Draco made his way along the catwalk, with Wulf behind to restrain him when he was about to kill one of the men from the other ship. In his madness, Draco still remembered his friend Wulf, though no other man was safe from him. There was a great satisfaction in the way the pirate helmets crunched beneath the oar stump.

From the now abundant supply on the slippery deck, Wulf had armed himself with a short cutlass and small shield. Donal had found himself a better ax and in his other hand held a javelin, which he was using for close-in stabbing. On the other ship, the old man in the green turban was pointing to the disturbance on the catwalk and calling orders to his men. The rain of missiles ceased falling on that part of *Fatima*.

Abu looked back from his station in the bow and for the first time saw the menace at his back. "The slaves are loose!" he shouted. He tapped several of his men who were not engaged against the boarders. "Come with me." They began making their way back toward the three rowers. The footing was extremely treacherous now, the planking awash with blood and littered with corpses, fallen weapons, and bits of rigging, and abristle with the short javelins.

Two of Abu's men came at Draco, short swords held low and shields high. The weighty club flashed in a horizontal sweep from right to left that sent both men hurtling over the heads of the rowers and onto the deck of the other ship. There was cheering from that ship, as all those not actively engaged in the assault against *Fatima* followed the drama being acted out on the catwalk. The old man in the green turban seemed to be showing special interest.

The action was diminishing swiftly, as men from *Fatima* dropped their arms and fell to their knees, begging for mercy. One of those begging for mercy was Rustam the Magnanimous. Abu was alone now, and the attackers leaned on their arms to witness how this singular duel would turn out. Abu seemed not to notice his solitary state, as he had attention only for the wild-bearded and patently insane man before him. Draco was frothing at the mouth, bug-eyed and splattered with blood from head to foot. "Do you know where I'm going to put this, Abu?" Draco shrieked, shaking the oar stump at the overseer.

Very swiftly for a fat man, Abu ducked a swing of the club and danced back. He caught the handle of a fallen dagger between his toes and with a dextrous flick of his foot launched it toward Draco's face. Draco jerked his head aside to avoid the knife, and in that second Abu was within the sweep of his club and bringing the short sword up for the vertical gutting stroke called "the ballsplitter." Draco danced back, bringing the oar down horizontally to crotch level. Abu's short sword sank into the wood and held there. Falcon brought the oar butt across the crack into Abu's jaw and send him tumbling into the slave pit. The rowers swiftly began clawing at Abu.

"Hands off—he's mine!" shouted Draco. He gestured to Wulf and Donal, and each grasped an ankle and hauled Abu halfway out of the slave pit. Draco reached down and ripped away Abu's loincloth. While his friends held their former tormenter, Draco raised the oar stump overhead and brought it down like a spear, ramming its end between Abu's grossly obese buttocks. Abu's scream paled even the most hardened of the soldiers standing on the two ships. Then, with a display of strength that drew admiring mutters from the witnesses, Draco raised the gross body over his head and cast it into the water.

"That oar'll keep him afloat for hours," Donal chuckled. "Unless the sharks get him first."

Wulf nudged Draco. "Master, we're not free yet." Draco looked around. Wulf had not called him "master" since they had been sold onto the galley—the oar pits created a society of equals. On both ships, bowmen were aiming shafts at the three. Aboard the false merchantman, the old man with the green turban was gesturing for them to come closer. They walked over the ghastly deck to easy speaking distance. The old man studied Draco. The young man was a fearsome sight, but his eyes had cleared.

"I see you have recovered your senses," said the man, in an Arabic so cultured that Draco and Wulf had difficulty following it. They were used to the rough Arabic and Turkish of the camps and ships.

"It passes, oh master," Wulf said. "It strikes him but rarely."

"A fortunate thing for his fellow man," the old man commented. "I have never seen such strength. This man has been touched by Allah. Drop your weapons and come aboard my ship. You three men are wasted on the oars." Draco had said nothing as yet, but he was held spellbound by the man in the green turban. He had seen at close hand many of the greatest war leaders and churchmen of the Crusader kingdoms, but he had never seen such regal bearing and dignity in a man. *Here,* he thought, *is a man I could follow. This is a man worth loyalty and love.*

Aboard the other ship, they were doused with buckets of water and scrubbed with stiff brushes before being taken to see the master. It was their first bath in two years, and, crude as it was, they reveled in it, and in their freedom from the chains, filth, and degradation of the oar pit. The hopeless tangle of their hair and beards was too much for the ship's barber, so he sheared their hair close to the scalp and shaved their faces clean. Wulf was only a little over sixteen, and his beard was still thin, but Draco's dense black-and-white tangle called for some painful scraping. They were given clean trousers and shirts of cotton. All three felt reborn.

In the meantime, both ships were being cleaned and repaired, the wounded tended to and the dead tossed overboard. A huddled group of pirates was held under guard on the deck of the merchant ship. Among them was

Rustam, looking most sorrowful. Draco and his companions were conducted to the stern, where the master now sat on cushions laid on a raised dais. Behind him knelt his sword bearer. The sword this man held was singular, and Draco had never beheld its like before. It was curved, and much larger than the usual Saracen sword. Its handle was long enough for two hands, its long hilt was in the form of a crescent moon, and its pommel was a smaller crescent. Its sheath was covered with sharkskin and severely plain.

Rustam was led before the master and fell to his knees, bowing until his brow touched the deck. "I beg your mercy, oh Suleiman," he gasped out. "All men know the mercy of Suleiman the Wise."

"What do you know of mercy, Rustam?" the old man said. "Did you show mercy to the ship of Christian pilgrims which you attacked last year in violation of our treaties?"

"Lies, all lies concocted by my enemies, oh Suleiman!" Rustam wailed.

"And the shipload of believers bound for Mecca last month, was that when you displayed mercy, Rustam?"

"Yet more lies! I have never harmed a believer, much less holy pilgrims, Suleiman!"

"Is this a lie?" Suleiman held forth a book, richly bound in gold and jewels. "This is a Holy Koran, and it belonged to the Lady Lilah, daughter of the Emir Jussuf bin Ali. She sailed from Alexandria for the *haj* aboard the *Sultana*. Neither ship nor pilgrims have been seen since."

"I got it in a trade, Suleiman. In port, I traded a jeweled sword for it. I swear it, oh Suleiman."

"Let us ask a disinterested party," Suleiman said. "Bring those three Franks to me." To Saracens, all Europeans were Franks. Falcon, Wulf, and Donal came to stand before Suleiman. "Be assured," Suleiman said, "that what you answer to my questions will have no bearing upon your future treatment, for good or ill. I but seek the truth in this matter. Did your ship within recent weeks attack a ship bearing pilgrims upon the *haj?*"

"It did," Draco said. His Arabic was halting but clear. "Rustam plundered the ship and turned the women and boys over to his men. When they were finished, all were killed, and the ship scuttled and sunk."

"He lies, oh Suleiman!" Rustam wailed, casting his turban on the deck and tearing his garments. "Would you take the word of an unbeliever against one of the faithful? It is unlawful!"

"This is not a holy court, Rustam," said Suleiman. "I am an official commissioned to root out pirates, and I am empowered to carry out justice as I see fit. Your men will be taken ashore, to be tried individually as their cases merit. You deserve no such consideration." The old man nodded to the man who knelt behind him. The man stood and drew the long sword. Draco noted that its blade was strangely and beautifully mottled. It was a Damascus blade! Draco had never seen one so large. The forging process was so complicated that most Damascus blades were to be found on daggers or short swords. Two men took Rustam's arms and dragged him to the rail. With an almost casual sweep of the beautiful blade, the sword bearer lopped off his head and the body was pitched overboard. The sword bearer wiped the blade with a piece of cloth. "A better death than he ever gave to his victims, master," he said.

An elderly officer in a gilded breastplate leaned toward Suleiman. "It must be a grief to you to soil Three Moons with the blood of such filth."

"Three Moons is just a sword," Suleiman said. "Merely a sharp piece of steel. If she makes man's lot a little better by ridding the world of such a one, what nobler purpose could she serve?" His officers and men nodded at their master's sage words. "Bring the Franks forward."

Draco and his companions sat on the deck before the

old man. Suleiman studied Draco for several long moments. "I took you for an older man," Suleiman said to Draco, "because of the white in your hair and beard, but you are little more than a boy. What are you called?"

"Draco de Montfalcon, master."

"Draco," mused Suleiman. "The word means 'dragon' in Latin. Did you know that?"

"No, I did not," Draco confessed. "It's a common name in my country."

"So, now I must decide what to do with you. I understand that that was the famous Abu of the Whip whom you killed so colorfully?"

"It was, master." Draco could not suppress a slight smile. Whatever happened next, the killing of Abu would warm his heart for as long as he lived, be his life long or short.

"I cannot condone cruelty," Suleiman said. "However, much may be forgiven one who has suffered at the hands of such a creature as Abu. In your use of the oar, to which you were chained, applied to that orifice of which Abu was so fond in other men, I detect a certain crude justice which is commendable despite its uncivil aspect." Suleiman's men made sounds of appreciation of Suleiman's famed justice.

"Young Draco," the old man said, "are you a knight?"

"I was to be knighted, master," Draco answered. "But I was captured after Hattin."

"No matter," Suleiman said. "You may become something better than a knight, in time." Draco was mystified at this. What could be better than being a knight?

"These two with you—are they friends?"

"The one with yellow hair was my horse handler, and we have been slaves together. The scarred man is from a place called Ireland where the folk are barbarous, but he is a fine warrior, as you saw, master."

"To hear a Frank speak of others as barbarous is a

wonder surpassing expectation, but I will agree that he seems a worthy man. You all seem good men. Will you take the *Islam?*" Draco knew this word to mean "submission," and it was how Moslems described their faith. "It is not difficult, but it requires sincerity. All that is necessary is that before believers"—he gestured to himself and his men—"you recite the words, 'There is no God but God, and Mohammed is his prophet.'"

Draco shook his head. "I am sorry, master. I am a Christian. My friends may decide for themselves." Wulf shook his head likewise. After a pause for thought, so did Donal.

"Well," said Suleiman at length. "If men cannot find it in their consciences to accept the *Islam,* it is good that they choose to stand by the faith of their ancestors. For has the Prophet not proclaimed the Christians and Jews to be People of the Book?" His men made ritual agreements that these were, indeed, the Prophet's words.

"Go and make yourselves useful about the ship, Franks," Suleiman said. "When we reach port, I will take you into my service. You will not be set to the oar again. I think that you have other possibilities."

For those words, Draco vowed that he would serve this man as he had served no other.

FOUR

"**Y**OUR sleep was troubled last night," Lilitha said. She spooned porridge into a wooden bowl and handed it to Falcon.

"It often is," Falcon said. "I've had a troubled life, and it comes to haunt me at night." He scooped up porridge on two fingers and popped it into his mouth. These villagers probably lived on porridge most of the year. Like their beer, it was made from barley, and it had been sweetened with honey.

"Life is slow here," Lilitha said. "Each year is like the last, and everything I do is just as my ancestors have done. But we sleep well at night."

"Be glad of it," Falcon said. He watched the woman chop greens. Her knife was of wood, with a thin piece of iron set into its edge. It was a poor country.

"Will one of your men lead me to the black riders' lair now? It's light enough."

"I've sent for the man you need. He's a hunter and knows this land better than any. I will visit some other villages in this valley and tell them what you have told me."

"Do that. Tell them that there is little time."

The man who arrived to guide him was small, like most of the men Falcon had seen here. His clothes were of brown wool and he carried a short wooden bow. The woman spoke to him at some length in the local language, of which Falcon could not understand a single word. Without a word, the man turned and left the house, and Falcon followed. He felt the woman's eyes on his back as he went.

They rounded up the rest of Falcon's men, and the guide took them uphill toward the pass between the twin peaks by a near-invisible game path. It was a long climb up steep slopes, and even though the men had discarded their armor for the expedition, they found it tiring work. In recent months, they had become more accustomed to riding than to marching.

By midday, they were concealed behind rocks overlooking the former abbey. Falcon studied the structure closely. It was far older than he had expected. The abbey had been built upon the still-standing walls of a much earlier building. Their hiding place was less than fifty paces from the massive walls, but there seemed to be no lookouts posted upon the newly erected battlements.

"I've seen brickwork like that before," Falcon said. The bricks of the lower walls were small and lozenge-shaped, set in a reticular pattern. "Before this was an abbey, it was a Roman fort. This pass must have been important to them." That would explain the path carved into the stone wall of the gorge. "They built well, those Romans. It wouldn't be easy to storm this place."

"The walls aren't high," observed Donal. "A quick rush with ladders could do the trick."

"Why is it built where enemies can get so close?" asked Rhys ap Gwynneth. "At this range, I could feather the eye slots on their helmets."

"Maybe their enemies had nothing but swords and javelins in those days," hazarded Simon.

"I'd like to get a look inside," Falcon said. The others looked at him with bewilderment.

"And just how would you be accomplishing that, my lord?" said Donal.

"They might want news of the outside world," Falcon said. "I could pose as a troubador."

"Begging my lord's pardon," Donal said, "but you sing like an ox with a bellyache."

"A merchant, then," Falcon said.

"They get all they need by raiding," Wulf pointed out. "They'd just kill you as they have everybody else they encounter except the people hereabouts. Besides, de Beaumont would know you in an instant."

"Would he?" Falcon said, still unwilling to give up the idea. "He's thought me dead for more than ten years. When he last saw me I was a boy."

"Master," Wulf said patiently, "there is no way in any guise, that those devils would allow you out of that place alive. You've always opposed foolhardiness in others. Don't give way to it yourself."

Falcon sighed. "You're right, I suppose. Still . . ." He gazed at the fortress with slitted eyes. Wulf knew well what Draco was thinking. Over there, just beyond those walls, sat one of the four men they had dedicated their lives to destroying. One of the men who had turned Falcon's father into a mass of torn, bleeding, suffering flesh. "We've seen all we can from here," Falcon said abruptly. "Let's go back."

On the way back to the village, Falcon was silent for a long time. At last he spoke to Wulf in a low voice. "Do you think that Valdemar was telling the truth, Wulf?" It was not the first time Wulf's master had brooded over that question.

"When did Valdemar ever tell the truth?" Wulf said.

"No, your father's dead. No man could have survived what we saw in Valdemar's castle." Gunther Valdemar had been one of the four traitors. The year before, Falcon had caught up with him and killed him, but before the man had died, he had said that Eudes de Montfalcon, Draco's father, had not died in the torture chamber of the castle near Hattin, and that Valdemar knew where he was. If it had been a lie to avenge his own death, then the German knight's vengeance was terrible. The thought that the traitors might be keeping his father alive somewhere tormented Falcon day and night.

They returned to the village famished. One of the Welshmen had shot a small mountain goat on the trek back, and a village woman prepared it for them. The tough, gamy meat was a welcome relief from the blandness of the usual fare. The villagers had no seasonings except local herbs, and salt was too precious to use except most sparingly. Falcon, accustomed to the plentiful spices of the East, was growing weary of the monotonous round of bread, cheese, and porridge, not that this interfered with his appetite in any way.

Falcon returned to Lilitha's house. She was still away, and he lay down on his pallet and fell to brooding upon the problem of the fort. How was he to take it without his army? Even if he could secure the people of the region as allies, they were not warlike and would have little chance against de Beaumont's mad knights. If he could send for his men, they could make short work of the place, but they might be campaigning all summer, and by the end of summer, the Crusaders even now assembling in the lowland would have scoured the district. It would have to be a work of craft rather than force.

Lilitha found him thus brooding when she returned. He looked and saw her frame against the light of the doorway, her black hair spangled with tiny spring flowers of many colors. A belt of plaited leather drew her woolen dress tight against her narrow waist, and Falcon remembered her as he had first seen her; her regal stance, the whiteness of her skin broken by the dense, startlingly black nest that covered her lower belly. For an instant, he felt a surge of the powerful desire that had come upon him during the pagan ceremony, then it passed.

"You look ready for a festival," Falcon said.

She touched the flowers in her hair. "It's our custom at this time of year." She came in and began building up the fire. The sun was getting low and the light was reddening. "When did you learn at the old Christian place?"

"That it'll be difficult to attack. That they may be mad, but they know how to build fortifications. It's unfortunate that we're so few. My engineer, Rupert, could have that place down around their heads in a day. As well wish for a host of angels, though. Did you have any luck with your neighbors?"

While she mixed dough and then kneaded it, she told him of her day among the other villages. She was a person held in esteem, but the mountain people were independent and would make no decisions until there had been much debate and argument, with every last villager having his say. Moreover, they were not inclined to take the word of outsiders.

Lilitha shaped the dough into a flat loaf. Brushing the glowing embers of the fire aside, she laid the loaf on the flat stone and raked the coals around it. She set a pot of stew over the flames. It was almost dark outside now, but the evening was warm, and the open fire made the room warm as well as smoky. Kneeling by the fire and stirring the pot, Lilitha casually freed the bone pegs that held her dress at the shoulders. The heavy garment fell slowly, stopped for a moment at her large, dark nipples, then dropped to pool around the rich swell of her hips. The rhythm of her stirring did not falter. The gesture seemed completely unself-conscious.

The sight disturbed Falcon more than it should have. He had grown up in crowded castles, where privacy had not even been a concept. Even among the highest nobility, wellborn young women commonly attended knightly guests in the bath. Still, the sight of the woman's body, even in its unprovocative pose, stirred him.

He found himself comparing her to others, women he had loved in the past. Was she as beautiful as Marie de Cleves, or Miriam, old Abraham's daughter? It was, he thought, like comparing a sword with a spear, or France with Outremer. This was a village wise woman, her body mature, womanly, voluptuous, primal with the pagan earthiness of her race. Marie had been very young and slender, the illiterate daughter of a simple country nobleman.

And Miriam? Falcon's heart ached at the memory. Her face and figure swam into his mind. The cultured daughter of one of the world's most formidably learned men, her hair had been as long and as black as Lilitha's, her body as full, but her unbelievably soft skin had been olive, and her voice had been as light and melodious as a songbird's, unlike Lilitha's low huskiness. Falcon turned his thoughts away from Miriam. It was too painful.

"Don't let your people debate too long," Falcon said, but his mind was not on his words. With every circuit of the wooden spoon, her breasts swayed from side to side. Falcon sat, hypnotized by the rhythmic movement, unable to look away and feeling increasingly foolish. She broke the spell by getting up and dipping out a bowl of ale, then stepped on silent feet around the fire and handed Falcon the bowl. Her hand rested on his for a long moment. She smelled like woman and wool and smoke.

Lilitha went back to stirring the pot. The loaf was browning and releasing a savory smell. She began to croon a song in time to her stirring in the unknown tongue. *Is she bewitching the brew?* Falcon thought. He took a drink of the ale. He had to say something to release himself from her spell.

"What herb do you put in the ale?" he said, irrelevantly. "What makes it bitter?"

"Wild hops," she said, with her eyes on her stirring and a secret-holding smile on her lips. "It preserves the ale, and it makes you drowsy. Had you noticed?"

Falcon nodded. So that was why he had felt so sleepy last night. He had never tasted hopped ale before. Gracefully, she rose and brought him a bowl of the thick stew. She broke the brown loaf in two and handed him half. The bread almost scorched his fingers, but she held hers as if it were cool. Lilitha reached to a bag dangling from a rafter overhead. She had to stand on tiptoe, and the gesture raised her breasts and sucked her mounded belly in beneath her ribs, so that she looked like some of the old pagan statues Falcon had seen in his travels, the ones old Abraham had said represented goddesses and the concept of victory. This woman seemed to do the most prosaic things with grace and surety. Falcon had known queens and duchesses who would have envied her poise.

The bag contained the inevitable goat cheese and Lilitha set it on the ground between them. She knelt next to Falcon, so that their knees touched. Falcon tore off a chunk of the bread, dipped it into the bowl, and bit into it. The stew was so laden with herbs that he could not tell what was in it. He ate heartily and without fear. If there was witchcraft in the woman, there was no evil, of that he was certain. When he had finished, she refilled his bowl with ale.

"Where is your home?" she asked. Her eyes were heavy-lidded and smoky.

"I have no home," he answered. "I had one once, but no more. That was in Normandy. That's far north of here, on the sea." He stared into the fire for a while. "Now my home is where my men are."

47

"Do you have a wife and children?"

"No wife, and no children that I know about." The thought of Miriam stabbed him for a moment, then vanished.

"That is sad. A man should have a woman, and he should breed children, many children. So many of them die."

"Do you have children?" Falcon asked uncomfortably.

"Three. But none lived." Her eyes locked on his, and he felt himself sinking into them. "You are tall," she said. "You would make tall sons and daughters." She loosened her belt, leaned forward to put her hands on his shoulders. He put his hands on her waist and slowly pulled her to him. She knelt upright and her dress fell to her knees, and Falcon felt a trembling in the pit of his stomach. Her face was an inch from his when they heard the beat of hoofs outside.

Falcon snarled a curse and released Lilitha. He jumped to his feet, and as he did a sudden dizziness made his head swim. He shook his head to clear it and snatched up his sword. There was no time to put on his armor. He clapped on his helmet and rushed outside. Wulf rushed to his side, and then the Welshmen arrived with bows strung and arrows nocked.

Men were riding into the village, men in black mail, with black shields. Some carried torches, and by their light Falcon could see that these were like the ones he had killed. The face-covering helmets revealed only inhuman blankness. All had fantastic crests.

The villagers boiled out of their doorways and milled uncertainly. Donal and Simon found Falcon, and his group stood together professionally: close enough together to present a united front, far enough apart to use their weapons freely.

A man with a snarling dragon's head atop his helm rode among the villagers. "There are outsiders here!" he shouted. "Give them to us or your village will be burned. We'll kill everything that lives down to the last rat!"

"We're not theirs to give!" Falcon called. "If you want us, we're right here, but I warn you we won't come along easily."

Wulf sighed wearily. "Apt at negotiation as always, my lord," the Saxon said.

The dragon-crested man looked all around him. In the head-covering helmet, he could not tell where the voice was coming from, and the vision slots restricted his sight.

"Men who don't fight with their heads in buckets know where their enemies are!" taunted Donal. A man with a coiled snake atop his helm said something and pointed. All the faceless heads turned toward the little group of armed men. They wheeled their horses and walked them slowly toward Falcon.

Falcon turned to Wulf and said, in Turkish: "There are too many. If we're separated, we meet at sunrise where Gower shot the goat." Wulf nodded and whispered the message to the others. The black riders stopped when they were within easy speaking distance.

"Who are you and why are you here?" asked the dragon-crested leader. His words were so muffled by his helmet that they were difficult to follow.

"If you'll take the pot off your head we'll be able to hear you better," Falcon said.

"Answer me!" the man bellowed. Falcon looked around. He saw that Lilitha had redonned her dress and stood before her house. He hoped that she would have the wit to flee the village as soon as fighting commenced.

"And who are you?" Falcon called. "By what right do you come here to take us? By what law do you demand our names and our business?" The questions were, of course, rhetorical, a way to buy time and study his enemy more closely before committing himself to violence. Draco Falcon knew full well that there was no right and no law in western Christendom save those of force and strength. To his great surprise, though, he received an answer.

"We are the knights of the Black Pope!" screamed the leader. "We are the servants of the Vicar of Hell! Our Dark Lord has promised us dominion of all the world, and it is by his authority that we order you to come with us!" The other riders shouted and rattled their spears against their shields.

"Mad as Donegal fleas," muttered Donal. The line of horsemen ambled forward, as if there were no need for haste. Abruptly, the two Welshmen raised their bows and and shot. The range was no more than ten paces, and the arrows from the terrible bows pierced the tough mail as easily as if it were cloth. The leader and another knight toppled from their mounts with the shafts protruding from their backs. The Welsh brothers faded back, nocking fresh shafts.

The fight in the village was furious but short. Fighting on foot, Falcon and his men were quickly scattered by the weight and bulk of the warhorses. The flickering torchlight lit the scene luridly as Falcon saw Donal's ax flash upward beneath a shield to crunch into a black-mailed side, saw the spiked ball of Simon's morningstar loop over another shield to smash a shoulder, then he was too busy with his own affairs to take much notice of what was happening around him.

The serpent-crested man rode down on Falcon, swinging a broad blade. Falcon swept the curved sword upward against the man's wrist, where the mail ended. Hand and sword dropped away, spattering Falcon with a spray of blood.

He had no idea where his men were now, and he concentrated on cutting his way out of the village and into the cloaking darkness beyond. Afoot and unarmored as he was, he did not try to fight armored horsemen on even terms. Instead, he cut at wrists, knees, stirrup leathers, or anywhere else that a mounted man was vulnerable.

A horse stumbled in the darkness, and Falcon leaped over it. The rider was struggling to his feet. Even the fine Damascus blade of his incomparable sword would be badly mangled by carving through the thick iron of the pot helm, so he clubbed the man behind the neck with the heavy crescent pommel. The black knight crumpled, and Falcon made a dash for the trees. His legs were strangely wobbly, and he was as short of breath as if he had been fighting a battle for hours. He knew what was coming, and he dreaded it.

Before the dizziness overwhelmed him, he sat and leaned his back against a tree trunk. The chills started, then the racking cramps and nausea. It was the old sickness that he had contracted in Outremer. It always came back, usually at the most inopportune times.

Oddly, the last thought to pass through his mind before passing out was: *Well, I wouldn't have been much use to her tonight anyway.*

The black riders found him there at dawn. They threw him across a pack horse, limp as a sack of grain. They picked up the beautiful sword and carefully wiped off the night's moisture, then wrapped it in cloth. As they rode toward the ancient abbey-fort, they paid no attention to Falcon's constant, delirous muttering.

Draco followed his new master through the narrow alleys of the bazaar. It bothered the young Frank that Suleiman had dismissed his bodyguard for the day and retained only Draco and Wulf to carry his books and writing materials as he walked about the city, from court to mosque to marketplace, dispensing justice, praying, and chatting volubly with high and low alike. Draco and Wulf were both distinctly uncomfortable at the thought of the old man thus exposing himself. Suleiman was a man much beloved of the people, but he was a man of power and prestige. Like all such men, he had many enemies.

Draco eyed the crowd nervously, one hand gripping the handle of the short sword Suleiman had given him. Wulf was likewise alert. Both young men were now clean-shaven, their hair beginning to grow out from the stubble left by the barber's crude shipboard shearing. They were dressed in tunics and trousers and cloaks of bright cotton, and they wore soft short boots. Their swords and daggers were belted about their waists in sheaths of tooled leather. After the years aboard the galley, they were just beginning to feel used to walking again.

Suleiman stopped to speak with a man in the garments of a Koranic scholar. The old man had dismissed his swordbearer, and he wore Three Moons on a waist belt. The sword looked almost comically huge, for Suleiman was not a big man by Frankish standards, though tall for a Saracen. Draco knew that the old man was not exactly frail, but he thought it foolhardy of him to wander about in public thus. He was glad that he and Wulf had been permitted to bear arms for Suleiman's protection, for the old man had shown them more kindness than they had known in years. Even in the best of times, the upbringing of a youth of knightly rank was a brutal business, and the love he had felt for his father and the other men of his family had been heavily compounded with fear and re-spect for their sheer brute power. Eudes de Montfalcon had raised his son to survive in a savage world, and Draco had known little tenderness or coddling after his fifth year.

Suleiman and the scholar were standing by a public fountain in one of the more open areas of the bazaar. Two women, heavily veiled, were making their way through the throng toward the fountain with earthen jars balanced upon their heads. Hawkers cried their wares and slaves or poor men bore huge bundles of goods upon their shoulders from one place to another. A lemonade seller bore an elaborate brass urn on his back and sang the praise of his beverage. A blind beggar tapped his way with his staff in one hand and his bowl in the other, asking in a polite, dignified way for alms. Draco knew the bestowal of alms to be one of the obligations of the followers of Mohammed and that there was no shame in the beggar's profession. He paid little attention to these innocent specimens of city life. He was on the lookout for the suspicious.

Wulf pointed with his chin toward a group of men, camel drivers by the look of them, who were lounging around a coffee seller's stall. "Keep an eye on that lot," the Saxon said. "They're bandits, or I'm a Scotsman." Draco eyed the band. They were indeed a villainous-looking crew, and it seemed to him that they were casting surreptitious looks at Suleiman. He wondered whether he should warn his master. He turned in time to see the old man reaching for the purse that hung next to his sword hilt, to give a few coins to the beggar. The beggar dropped his bowl, and before it hit the ground, there was a long, curved dagger in his hand. The thing had happened so swiftly that Draco could only gape, knowing that Suleiman would die within the next second.

What happened next seemed to take place with extreme slowness, as if his perceptions were altered, as they had been the time he and some other squires had tried hashish on a dare. Suleiman's hand, instead of dipping in his purse, grasped the long hilt of Three Moons. The bright blade flashed from the scabbard in a glittering arc that passed through the "beggar's" throat when the dagger was still an inch from Suleiman's ribs. The single sweep of the sword carried it high above the old man's shoulder, and then he was gripping it in both hands as the women dropped their jugs and snatched daggers from their

53

garments. The sword came downward across the shoulder of the nearest, cutting to the waist on the opposite side.

Draco had dropped his box of books and was midway throught the act of drawing his sword, still stupid and aghast at the sudden turn of events. *He moves so slowly!* Draco thought. *His blows have so little force! The next one must kill him!* The second veiled killer was moving in as the big blade came up almost lazily. There seemed something blurry about the move, and Draco could not quite see the track of the blade, but the veil divided upward, parting to reveal a bearded, grimacing face. Then a red line split the face from chin to brow and the man toppled, spraying blood from a head that had been cleft halfway through. As he fell, Draco saw that the "beggar" had not yet quite finished collapsing. It was then that Draco realized that Suleiman's movements had been so perfectly timed that they only *seemed* slow, so precise that blows which would have severed a horse's head had actually appeared to be weak. What he had seen was absolute perfection of the swordsman's technique.

For an instant, all motion and sound froze, then all was bustle and chaos. Draco and Wulf broke from their paralysis and dashed to the old man's side, their weapons now clear. Suleiman eyed the swords with some amusement. "A little late for that, don't you think?"

"There may be more, master," said Draco, trying to hide his chagrin.

"I think not. As bodyguards, you two make passable clothes racks." The young men flushed with shame. They had stood by like idiots while this man of grandfather's years had dealt with the threat alone.

"Were they Hashishin?" asked the scholar to whom Suleiman had been speaking when the attack began.

"They were," said Suleiman. Draco and Wulf eyed the corpses with horror. The Hashishin, the hashish eaters, were the fanatical followers of the Old Man of the Mountain, who sent out his killers from his castle at Alamut to murder the enemies of his sect, whether they be Christian or Moslem. The Crusaders had corrputed the name of the sect to Assassins.

The old scholar chuckled dryly. "When will they learn, oh Suleiman, that you cannot be taken unawares?"

"All men are mortal, Hassan, and the day of my death is written upon my brow, like that of other men. When Allah wills it, I shall die, by the hand of a hashish eater or some other way." He handed the bloody sword to Draco. "Clean her."

Draco took the weapon. It was the first time he had held it, and the experience was a revelation. To him, accustomed to the broad, straight chopping swords of Europe, the curved, long-hilted sword called Three Moons had appeared awkward and clumsy. Now that he held it, he knew that its balance was perfect for the kind of swift cutting for which it was designed. He cut a piece of veil from one of the dead Assassins and the cloth parted so cleanly that it felt as if the blade had passed through empty air. As he wiped the blood from the blade with the piece of cloth, the sword seemed to come alive in his hand, to call to him to strike out at something, and he wondered if the blade was bewitched.

"I told you to clean Three Moons, not to practice with her," said Suleiman. Flushing, Draco handed the sword back, not without reluctance. He saw that the old man was regarding him with a kind of calculation.

As they walked back to Suleiman's spacious town house, he lectured them. "How was it that you two did not see the killers? Why were you watching those caravaneers?" How had he known that? His back had been to them.

"They looked wicked, master," Wulf said.

"Poor men often do," Suleiman observed. "And why did you pay no attention to the blind beggar or the

55

women with water jugs?" The voice was patient, pedantic, but it carried a chilling edge.

"Who ever notices such?" Draco asked.

Suleiman sighed. "Like most men and like all Franks you go through the world half blind, seeing only the most obvious. Nothing that is beyond the reach of your sword impinges upon your consciousness." The young men listened intently, striving to understand the unfamiliar words.

"How does a blind man walk?" the old man asked suddenly.

"Slowly, and with hesitation," Draco answered.

"Quite true, and that beggar was walking with a great deal *too much* hesitation for one who has been blind for years. Does a woman's walk not differ from a man's?" Draco thought hard. The two false women had been walking with a perfectly feminine hip sway.

"They walked like women, master," Draco said.

"Yes, they waggled their bottoms like Cairo whores. That is *not* the way a woman walks when she is balancing a jar upon her head. Then, she places each foot carefully before the other and her shoulders stay level and her hips scarcely sway at all."

"Then," Draco said, "you were prepared for the attack even before you began speaking with the imam?"

"I have been prepared for attack since my father first put Three Moons in my hands."

That night, in the little room he and Wulf shared, Draco went over the events of the day. How could a man know so much and be so skillful? Had Suleiman really known that the "women" were actually men in disguise, or had he only said that to appear more sagacious than he was? Draco rejected that thought. Suleiman had great pride, but he had no vanity.

Draco ran the sequence of events through his mind

again and again, striving to find the key to this riddle. Then he had it. The sword had flashed out of its sheath and through the throat of the "beggar" in such wise that, at the end of the stroke, the blade had been in perfect position for the cut against the first "woman." It had been so positioned *before* they had dropped their jugs. It made the fighting of Frankish knights, for which Draco had trained so many long, hard years, seem like the play of children.

Without waking Wulf, Draco left the room and sought out Suleiman. He found the old man in his study, seated upon a cushion and reading from his treasured Koran. Three Moons was laid upon her stand near his right hand. Without looking up, Suleiman gestured for Draco to seat himself upon a cushion. The old man read awhile longer, then closed the book. He looked at Draco. "I was expecting you. You want me to teach you to fight as you saw me fight today."

"Yes, master." Was the old man able to read minds?

"And for what reason, other than the usual Frankish fascination with better ways to kill?"

"There are certain men I must kill, master. I have dedicated my life to this."

"These will be the murderers of your father, of whom you spoke when you first accepted service with me. It is a man's duty to avenge his father's death. I avenged the death of my father. But this may be done without the kind of teaching you request. You Franks kill crudely but efficiently."

"It is more than that, master," Draco said, searching for words. "I wish to be a man like you." Suleiman regarded the young man for a long time before speaking again.

"The training is arduous. And if you would be a whole man, you must be more than a mere killer. You must learn the arts of civilization, from me and from the doctor

Abraham of Toledo. You are old to be starting, and you must work hard if you would bear Three Moons after me."

Draço was stunned. "B-but, master," he stammered, "surely it must be your own son who takes her from your hands."

"My sons are dead, killed by your Crusaders and by enemies who profess the *Islam*." He said these words without bitterness. "I am glad that you have come to me, my boy. I know that my sons' deaths were foreordained by Allah, but in the weakness of my faith I cannot but feel that they would have outlived me if I had taught them better. Perhaps Allah has granted me the chance to atone for my failure."

FIVE

HUGO de Beaumont, once an archbishop of Holy Mother Church, now the self-styled Black Pope, sat in his cathedra throne with a shirt of mail across his knees. He was a huge man, with a great hill of belly, three chins, wide jowls, and a round, merry, pink-cheeked face. Just now he was dressed all in black robes, and a black miter stood atop a chest in a corner of the large, neat room.

He gazed with wonder upon the mail hauberk. It was made of many thousands of tiny rings, each ring passed through four others and its ends flattened and closed with a minute rivet. It was Saracen mail, beyond a doubt, but in all his years in Outremer, de Beaumont had never seen any as fine. In Europe, the knights wore mail of exactly the same construction, but the rings were made of hammered wire, and the iron was softer than that made in the East. This was clearly made of drawn wire as hard as sword steel. Despite its Saracen make, the hauberk was of European design, though it weighed perhaps a third as much as a European hauberk of similar proportions. De Beaumont fondled the metal mesh sensuously, the fabric so fine that it slithered and flowed between his fingers like silk.

He turned his attention to the helmet that stood on his desk. He picked it up and turned it between his hands. It was rather tall and conical, its pointed top canted slightly forward. It had a broad, flaring noseguard that was curved to cover the sides of the nose as well as the bridge. It was the type of helmet worn for many centuries by European knights but now regarded as rather old-fashioned; it was being replaced by head-covering helms such as his own men wore. Still, many experienced warriors preferred the superior vision and hearing provided by the old design. The graceful fluting of its sides betrayed its Saracen manufacture. It, too, was extremely light and strong.

Finest of all was the sword, which lay glittering on the desk. This was of purely Saracen design, though it was larger than any European sword of de Beaumont's experience. He had handled it, savored its perfect balance. He had even considered belting it to his side, but in the end he had put it away. He was too used to his club, standing now in the corner. It was the same oaken cudgel he had taken with him to Syria, so many years before, but now its knotty head bristled with cruel spikes, for he was no longer bound by his vows not to shed blood.

"Marco," de Beaumont called. A big man entered, dressed in iron mail blackened by coating it with oil and baking it in an oven. He was the captain of de Beaumont's knights, and he had shaggy brown hair and a large mustache. "My lord?" the knight inquired.

"What do you make of this gear, Marco?"

"It's the finest I've ever seen," said the knight, his French tinged with the accents of Lombardy. "We found it in the hut of the one the villagers call the Old Woman. The man we brought in had the helmet and the sword, so the mail must be his also, though where a sell-sword like that got such princely equipment I can't guess."

"That sell-sword is no ordinary man. Bring us some wine, Marco." The Lombard knight poured red wine from a pitcher into two golden cups and handed one to his master. The cups were chalices looted from churches.

"I know he can't be ordinary. Afoot and without his mail he killed or crippled five men last night. His men aren't ordinary footmen, either. They all fought like knights, and two of them had bows that could pierce mail. I'd wager my head that these fellows had something to do with the seven men who didn't return from the last raid."

"He's more than you think, and if the Southern sickness hadn't laid him low, he'd have accounted for even more of our men."

"Do you know him, my lord?"

"Yes, though I'd thought him dead many years ago. I knew him at once by the white streak in his hair and the scar that runs from his brow to his heel. In Outremer I knew him as Draco de Montfalcon. He was just a boy then, though he fought as well as any knight. His father was my friend Eudes de Montfalcon."

"How did he come by the marks, my lord?" asked Marco, intrigued.

"It's a strange tale," said de Beaumont, cradling his winecup and settling back into his chair. He loved to tell stories, and told them as well as any professional jongleur. Marco knew this well, and he relished good tales as well as any man. In the cramped, dank castles of Europe, men had little to do in winter except entertain each other with stories and songs.

"Some of this I had from Eudes," de Beaumont began. "Some I heard from others, though Draco himself would never speak of it. It happened on the last leg of their journey to Outremer. Eudes and his household had taken ship from Constantinople. As the ship passed Cyprus, it was set upon by Cypriot pirates. As you might imagine, a shipload of Crusaders were no easy prey, and the fight was fierce. Eudes clove many, for he was a mighty man. Draco would have been about fourteen, but he fought well.

"In the midst of the fray, a storm blew up, accompanied by lightning. It was such lightning as none there had ever seen. The bolts were blue and they went crawling among the waves and each bolt hissed along for many seconds before winking out. Instead of breaking off the engagement, as is customary when a storm interrupts a sea battle, the uncanny lightning seemed to drive all the men into a mad blood-frenzy and they fought and killed with redoubled fury." De Beaumont paused in his recitation and took a drink of his wine. Marco drank and waited for the rest with a mounting fascination.

"The lightning began to come aboard the ships," the former prelate continued. "Wherever it touched a man, it killed. Draco and Eudes had been separated in the fighting, and the boy stood with his back to the mast, hewing away, stalwart as any knight in Christendom." At the mention of Christendom, both men made a peculiar hand gesture. "Just as Eudes had hacked his way back to his son, a great bolt came gliding like a dragon along the deck, slaying dozens. Each man as he was touched lit up like a midsummer bonfire and dropped to the deck, dead and smoking. Before flashing out like the others, the bolt struck Draco de Montfalcon squarely." De Beaumont paused for another swallow.

"They say that Eudes went berserk then, and that single-handed he slew the last of the Cypriot pirates, driving them back aboard their ship and following them onto it, hacking and smiting until there was nothing living aboard. I have heard that by the time the fight was finished his sword looked like an old saw, so many shields and helms had it cloven.

"Satisfied that he had wrought sufficient slaughter, Eudes went back aboard his ship to mourn his son and prepare him for burial. To his great surprise, the boy was still breathing, though badly burned and unconscious. He remained unconscious or in a raving delirium for many days, though eventually he recovered. He was the only man struck by the lightning who lived.

"Although the boy seemed to have recovered fully, he was always a little strange after that. He would spend days brooding like a rejected lover, then laugh endlessly over nothing, and sing and dance merrily even though there was plague and starvation in the camp. Sometimes he would go into mad rages, and then no man was safe from him, for at those times his strength was doubled, and he had been strong before. The only ones he would recognize at such times were Eudes and his horseboy, a Saxon from England whose name escapes me now. As he grew older, the spells grew less frequent, but they never entirely left him." De Beaumont paused for a long time, dwelling upon his thoughts.

"Spared by the lightning that killed the others," said Marco, awestruck. "Do you suppose he was consecrated to our Master?"

"No. If he had been, Eudes would have joined with me and the others when we asked him to. Instead, he tried to expose us, and refused to reveal the secret with which he was entrusted and which would have rendered us immune from all interference."

"That being?" Marco queried, slyly.

"That is not for you to know," said de Beaumont sternly. "Anyway, we put Eudes to the question in Valdemar's castle near Hattin. Somehow Draco suspected what was happening, and he sneaked into the castle, along with the Saxon and a Saracen servant. They interrupted the questioning, though they could not rescue Eudes, then they fought their way out, though the Saracen was killed.

You would not believe how much destruction those two boys wrought." He chuckled, setting his jowls aquiver. "The Saxon lad even wounded that braggart fool Gerard de Ridemont, grand master of the Templars!"

"Gerard!" said Marco, startled. "He was there?"

"Of course," grumbled de Beaumont, as if he thought he had said too much. "And there were others, too, whose names would surprise you. Well, the boys got clean away, and it seems that they got back to King Guy's army, but too late to warn him, because Valdemar captured them when he was picking up stragglers after the battle of Hattin. He sold them onto a Turkish galley, and that was the last anyone heard of them, to my knowledge. I had presumed them dead, like any other man who pulls a Turkish oar."

"And Eudes?" asked Marco.

"You ask too many questions," said de Beaumont. Marco cursed inwardly. The Black Pope always turned silent just as he was about to reveal the really important secrets. Still, the man he had found helpless in the grip of malaria that morning had survived the terrible lightning that had killed all others it touched, and he had somehow survived the living hell of a Turkish galley. Just what kind of man was this Draco de Montfalcon?

Aethelwulf Ecgbehrtsson, commonly called Wulf, sat upon a rock, shivering and cursing in the early-morning cold. It had not been a good night. The black-haired girl in the village hut had just begun to claw at his back, moaning frantically, when the alarm had come from outside. She had cried her disappointment when he rolled from her body to snatch up his weapons and hose and dash outside into the bloody night.

Then there had been the chaotic battle through the village and the frantic, night-long hide-and-seek with the black riders, in and out through the stunted trees of the mountain forest. Wulf had shaken his pursuers and made his way to the agreed-upon rendezvous to find the Welshmen already there. Donal the Irishman and Simon the Monk had arrived soon. But where was Falcon?

"They have him," Donal said. The Irishman drove the edge of his ax several times into the ground to clean off the thick encrustation of blood that stained it. "Live or dead, they've taken him, else he'd be here."

"I don't believe it!" Wulf shouted. "No man could take my lord captive! I've seen him carve his way through a hundred such as we saw last night." He knew the Irishman was right, but he didn't want to admit it, even to himself.

"A hundred?" Donal said, cocking a split eyebrow. "And I thought we Irish had a reputation for stretching our feats. Look you, Wulf, any man can be taken. Draco's tougher than most, but consider: He had no armor, it was dark, and he must have been swiving the witch-woman crosseyed all evening. They have him, Wulf. We must face it and decide what to do."

Wulf was in anguish. He had not been separated from Falcon since his tenth year. In many ways, the two were more like brothers than like master and man. Now the others were looking to him for orders. Wulf was not used to thinking and planning. Falcon had always done that. He cracked his knuckles and tried to come up with a plan.

"We must find out whether he is alive," Wulf said at last. "If he's dead, then we will avenge him, but if he lives, we must find some way to free him."

"Someone comes," said Gower. The men fell sprawling to the ground, weapons ready. The Welshmen held their bows flat on the ground before them, arrows on string. Wulf raised his head slightly. On an open slope below them, he could make out two figures.

"It's that hunter who guided us yesterday," said Rhys. "The witch-woman is with him." From his movements, it was plain that the hunter was following their tracks and was swiftly closing the distance between them.

"Do you want us to kill them?" asked Rhys.

"Let's see what they want," Wulf said. "We can always kill them later." When the two came within speaking distance, Wulf stood up "Good morning, Old Woman. I hope you bring us good news, because we stand in need of some."

"I came to tell you your master is alive." The woman seated herself upon the ground, and the hunter crouched beside her, his eyes nervously scanning the five hardbitten men before them.

"Where is he?" Wulf asked, masking his anxiety behind the impassive façade of the warrior.

"In the black riders' place."

"How was he taken?"

"We don't know for sure. Some of my people saw the riders from hiding. Falcon did not seem to be injured. He was loaded across a pack beast, and he was tossing and muttering as if he were very sick."

"The Southern sickness!" Wulf said. "What a time for it to strike him!" Then, to the woman, "What did the rider do after we escaped?"

"Most of them went chasing you. Some stayed behind and demanded that we bring them all your goods and animals. They have your armor and your packs and bags." She gestured to a bundle carried by the hunter. "They overlooked the clothes you left behind in the huts where you were quartered. I've brought them." The men tore open the bundle and scrambled into the garments.

"Thank you, lady," Wulf said, when he was dressed and warm at last. "Why did the riders spare the village? I see no smoke."

"I cannot say. For all their wild threats they did nothing to us except to forbid us to harbor you again."

"Now, why might that be?" Wulf said. Ordinarily, any peasant village that offered knights the slightest defiance was burned as a matter of routine. Even without such provocation, villages were often destroyed just for fun.

"They seem to be humorless men," Donal observed. Then, in Turkish, "Or this could be treachery. They may have sold us to the riders in return for their lives. Best to kill them now."

"No," Wulf said, in the same tongue. "We need these people, if we're to get our lord's freedom. If they meant treachery they would have led the riders here." Wulf sat down on his rock and pondered. How would Draco handle this? He strove to think as his master would. What would Falcon do if Wulf were held prisoner in the black riders' fort?

"Do you think we could ransom him?" Simon asked.

"No," Wulf replied. "They don't make war like civilized men." At last, he came to a decision. "Lady, can you guide us back to the mouth of the river gorge so that we won't be seen?"

"Yes, I can do that. You won't be trying to free him, then?" She sounded disappointed.

"I didn't say that," Wulf said. "Lead us there."

"Ten of 'em," Donal said. From the edge of the treeline, they could see the band of black riders encamped near the monolith at the entrance of the gorge. They were dismounted, but fully armored, and their mounts were tethered nearby, shields hanging from their saddles.

"We can't get around them," Wulf said. "We'll have to kill them." He considered the problem. Five lightly armed and unarmored men on foot against ten mounted knights armed to the teeth and clad in iron from head to foot. It was a daunting prospect, but he'd faced worse before and come out alive. But then, Falcon had been in charge on those occasions.

"We stand a better chance if we wait until nightfall," Wulf said.

"We need good light to use our bows unless we get very close," Gower reminded him. Wulf bit back a curse. Falcon wouldn't have forgotten that.

"Can you kill them from here?" Wulf asked.

The Welshman shook his head. "It's two hundred and fifty paces at least. We can't pierce mail at such a range. We can kill their horses, though."

"We need the horses," Wulf said. "Well, no sense waiting. It'll be dark soon." He stood and readied his weapons, and the others did likewise. Lilitha had been sitting by them silently, and now she looked from one to another. They had been speaking a rough soldier's French that she could not follow.

"What will you do now?" she asked.

"We're going to go kill those men," Wulf answered. "If we succeed, come join us at the gorge. If we die, do as you think best."

The five men stepped boldly out into the open and began walking at a quick pace toward the ten horsemen. They did not run, because it is not good to begin a fight already out of breath. They had covered nearly one hundred paces before they were seen. There was a shout from the camp and the knights mounted and helmed themselves. They adjusted their shield straps and hefted their lances arrogantly and without haste.

Wulf smiled grimly. The black-mailed maniacs were going to make this easier than he had hoped. Horsemen were the same everywhere. They believed themselves to be lords of the earth and refused to take mere footmen as a serious threat. When they were ready, the horsemen began cantering toward the little band.

68

The Welshmen held their bows at full draw, and when the horses were fifty paces away they released. "Knights never learn," Gower said, as two men fell with arrows through the eye slots of their helms. Before the bowmen could shoot again, the riders were upon them.

Donal swept a lance aside with his ax and raised himself on tiptoes to smash the edge into the horseman's shoulder before the man could bring his shield across.

Simon dodged beneath the neck of a horse to come up on the rider's shield side. He slammed the shaft of his morningstar into the shield and the spike-studded ball looped over the defense on its chain, smashing into the back of the man's neck and snapping his spine.

Wulf rolled beneath a horse's feet, then sprang up astride its rump. Jerking back the knight's helmet, he thrust up beneath it with his falchion and felt his sword hand immediately inundated with a warm flood of arterial blood. He tumbled from the horse's rump in a back somersault that would have done credit to a tumbler and landed on his feet.

The Welshmen had run to one side as the line of horsemen drew near, and now, as it passed, they fired arrows into the exposed backs of two more. The three remaining riders were wheeling and cursing, unable to comprehend the massacre going on around them. One got his sword clear and took a swing at Wulf, but the Saxon easily avoided the heavy weapon and thrust upward beneath the skirts of the mail. The point took the man in the groin and ripped up, gutting him.

Simon got the chain of his morningstar around the wrist of a horseman and yanked the man from his saddle. As the knight scrambled to his knees, Donal took his ax in both hands and brought its edge in a roundhouse swing against the back of the black iron pothelm. Even the heavy ax would not split the thick metal but the blow was so powerful that the iron crumpled inward and blood shot from the eye slots.

One horsemen was left, and he kept wheeling his horse, trying vainly to keep all his enemies before him.

"Drop your weapons and yield," Wulf called. "We'll give you quarter."

"Yield?" shrieked the knight. "I'll die before I ask quarter of common filth like you!"

"As you will," Wulf said, and two arrows appeared less than an inch apart through the mail covering the man's throat. The Welshmen finished the wounded with their long knives as the others cleaned their weapons, then all pitched in to strip the dead and recover the arrows. The horses took some catching, but soon all were rounded up. Lilitha and the huntsman walked from the treeline to the scene of the slaughter. The sun was dipping behind the mountains and the sky was almost violet.

The woman looked at the sprawled, stripped bodies. "No one should be able to kill so easily," she said.

"We're warmen, lady," Wulf said. "It's a hard life and it makes hard men. At least we confine our killing to other soldiers. These were murderers, and mad to boot. If you'd seen the village in the lowland that I saw, you'd shed no tears for these." Wulf began going over the loot. He had hoped to salvage some gear that they could use, but little that the knights had carried was of any use. The mailcoats were long and heavy, and men who fought afoot had no use for the mail leggings. The shields and swords and lances were likewise heavy and awkward unless used from the saddle.

"What a heap of useless iron," Donal said, scratching his head. "If I had a good pair of nippers, I could cut these hauberks down to useful size." Like most soldiers, they felt exposed fighting without at least light body armor.

Lilitha eyed the horses. The booty was being bundled

and tied behind the saddles. "Are you leaving now?" she asked.

"Some of us," Wulf replied. "Simon, I have a task for you." The monk rode up on the horse he was trying out. The beast seemed content with the change of masters. "Ride from here," Wulf continued, "and find the army. Bring them here. All of them—men, siege gear, everything. If they have to break with that Savoyard, we'll settle with him later. This is more important." The others nodded agreement. Feudal duty came above all.

Simon eyed the narrow rock ledge dubiously. "I don't think the siege engines will make it up that path," the ex-monk said. "Not even disassembled. It's too narrow for carts."

"Rupert can do it," Wulf said. "You can't travel alone. Rhys, Gower, go with him. You two can shoot game if you come across no habitation. Take this gear, except for two of the lances. When you come to a big town, sell the armor. Use as much of the price as you need to get back to the army and turn the rest in to the war chest." Mail hauberks contained a great deal of iron and took thousands of hours of labor to complete. Even with a few holes in them, ten hauberks and ten pairs of mail leggings were worth a couple of good-sized villages, complete with inhabitants.

"What about you and Donal?" Simon asked.

"We'll stay and do what we can." Wulf looked nervously toward the treeline. "Go now. Leave us two horses, but ride. They may be sending a relief for these louts." Simon and the Welshmen rode away, grim-faced at the prospect of negotiating the narrow rock path in the dark.

Lilitha looked puzzled and Wulf explained what he had done. "You mean," she said, "that you two are staying here? What can you accomplish by yourselves?"

"I don't know yet," Wulf said.

"You must be madder than the black riders, then," Lilitha said. "Why do you do this?"

"Why, he's our lord," Donal said, as if that explained everything.

"And we're his men," said Wulf.

SIX

H E had been conscious for some minutes before he could remember what his name was. Falcon. Or maybe it was de Montfalcon, he wasn't sure. His vision was blurry and the light was dim as he strove to make out his surroundings. He was so weak that it was a serious effort merely to raise his head. To one side, he thought he could make out the diamond-shaped meshes of a net. Was he in a fisherman's hut? There seemed no reason for that. It certainly didn't smell like such a place.

What it smelled like was a dungeon. His memory was still faulty, but he knew that he had awakened in dungeons before. Bad as his situation seemed, he knew that it could be worse. It was better than waking to the sight of the whip-scarred back of a rower on the bench before him. He let his head fall back into the straw that covered the floor. At least that was no hardship. The floors of the castles he had been raised in had been straw-covered. He hadn't slept on a real bed until his fifteenth year, in Palestine. Even then his father had worried about the softening effects of such decadent luxury.

After an hour or more, he felt strong enough to roll

over. Then he spied a pitcher and a wooden trencher near a door. Slowly, he crawled over to them. When he had covered the ten or so feet, he had to stop and rest for several minutes before proceeding. The pitcher was full of pure spring water. He was suddenly conscious of a ravening thirst and had to force himself to drink slowly, careful not to let the pitcher fall from his shaking hands.

When his thirst was somewhat quenched, there was still half a pitcher of water left. He turned his attention to the trencher. Upon it lay a flat loaf of bread and a large piece of slightly moldy cheese. The coarse bread was a bit stale, but Falcon ate it all, breaking off small pieces and chewing each thoroughly, taking sips of water to help it down. When the bread was gone, he started on the cheese, first scraping the mold off against the thick, grainy wood of the door. When that was gone, he searched the trencher for crumbs and ate them all. He needed every bit of strength he could obtain. Besides, even the tiniest crumbs of food would attract vermin.

He dragged himself to a wall and sat with his back against it. He was still terribly weak, but he could already feel the strength returning with even such poor sustenance to work on. With the sickness past, his body's tremendous recuperative powers were coming back into play.

His memory was returning, too. As always after a siege of a recurring sickness, it was the events of the last few days that remained vague. Where was Wulf? Was he in another cell? The last thing he could remember was the ride to his little army's appointment with the Savoyard noble. Had he been captured in the fighting? He had a hazy memory of a massacred village, and there was something about men in fantastic helms. Maybe he was just confused. The butchery in the village might have been on the Crusaders' march through Hungary. He'd seen plenty of such slaughter then.

Then he remembered the net. He studied the wall opposite. What he had taken for a net was the pattern made by the brickwork of the wall, with small, square bricks set on edge, the mortar forming a reticular pattern. He recognized it as ancient Roman brickwork. Roman? Then the memories began flooding back and his bowels quaked as he realized who had him prisoner. Memories of the castle at Hattin and his father on the rack and the chains and hot irons. How long had he been here? He felt his face. The beard stubble was at least five or six days old. He knew from bitter experience that he needed several more days to regain his strength. How to survive those days?

Next his anguished thoughts returned to his men. Had they gotten away? He ardently hoped so. He was their lord and he had failed them. Bitterly, he cursed himself for his foolhardy behavior. He had let his lust for vengeance overrule his judgment and he had led his little band against impossible odds. Wulf had warned him. The Saxon was not very imaginative, but he was infinitely more practical. What was it old Suleiman had said? *If your Norman adventurousness, greed, and ferocity ever combine with the Saxon sense of logic and practicality, then surely the earth shall tremble.* Not much likelihood of that. The Saxons, like the Irish, were now a subject people under the Norman yoke.

He dragged his wandering thoughts back to mundane matters. How to survive? First off, he had to play for time and keep de Beaumont off his guard. From the food and water, they would know him to be conscious once more. At least, he could pretend to be out of his head for a while.

After that, any time he heard someone approaching, he tossed about on the floor, moaning and rolling his eyes. His appearance was wild enough to lend credibility to the act. He was wild-bearded and filthy, his skin was a shocking yellow from the malaria, and the white streaks in hair and beard gave him the incongruous look of some strange Biblical prophet.

The food was replaced at regular intervals, as was the water. His hard, enduring body was able to sustain itself on incredibly poor fare, but still he needed more to build up his strength. One night, he awoke with a large rat crouched upon his face. Moving as slowly as he could, Falcon opened his mouth and wiggled the tip of his tongue. As the rat poked its head inside to examine this fascinating morsel, Falcon bit down hard, breaking the rodent's neck. He tore the hide off the animal with his teeth and ate the flesh raw. He threw the hide and bones out of the two-inch slot in one wall which served as a window. He saved a few bits of offal as bait for more rats.

After that, he managed to eat at least one rat each day, and his body flooded with new strength from the meat. Rat was not his favorite food, but he ate it without revulsion. At the terrible siege of Acre, rats had been highly esteemed. If he ran short of rats, he could always eat the cockroaches. There were plenty of them.

Food was not enough. When he could be sure nobody was watching, he exercised, running in place or doing the routines Suleiman had taught him to keep his muscles and reflexes toned even though he had neither space nor arms to work with. His mind he did not need to exercise. It burned with hatred and shame and rage.

Sometimes he thought of Lilitha. He hoped she had not been killed and that her village was spared, but he had little basis for that hope. He tried not to think of her too much. Thoughts of women did a man little good in such a situation. More than anything else, he planned what he would say, how he would act, when he had to face de Beaumont.

De Beaumont studied his prisoner through the viewing slot in the dungeon door. The walls and rooms in this part of the fort were ancient, but all the doors had been re-placed in his renovations, and the door smelled pleasantly of fresh-cut timber. It was the only thing pleasant about the place. In the dim light of the cell, the man he had known as Draco de Montfalcon was not a pretty sight. Still, considering what he had been through, he looked better than he had any right to.

Draco had been thrown into the cell naked, and his long, rangy body was as lean and powerful as any de Beaumont had ever seen. His color was still yellowish, but improving. The bizarre white line from scalp to heel turned the hair white along its path, making white blazes at chest and crotch.

"He's looking better," de Beaumont said to Marco. "In fact, except for those white patches, he looks remarkably like my old friend Eudes."

"Most of the men have been down here to have a look at him," Marco said. "To see the mark of the lightning."

De Beaumont was annoyed, but he said nothing. The men were all superstitious louts, and he didn't want them holding Draco in some kind of awe. "Open the door," he ordered. Marco drew back the simple bolt that fastened the door from the outside. In this remote area, there were no skilled locksmiths to fashion proper dungeon fittings. But then, de Beaumont's men never took prisoners anyway. The circumstances of Falcon's arrival and capture had been freakish.

Falcon looked up, eyes dull, as de Beaumont entered.

"Well, young Draco," the former prelate said jovially, "I trust you are feeling better."

"Some," Falcon answered. "I've eaten better, though."

"Why, if you'd come freely, as a guest, you'd have had the best. Instead, you came stealthily, and you refused my invitation, and you killed my men."

Falcon shrugged. "They spoke to me discourteously.

77

What else is a man of honor to do? I could not let a slight go unanswered."

De Beaumont sighed. This was disappointing. The man talked just like any other brutish feudal noble. "But what brought you here, Draco? This is a remote place."

"I was at loose ends," Falcon said. "I'm a sell-sword now; no liege, no fealty. I go where there's work for my sword. I heard about this band of black-mailed raiders. They seemed to be prospering, so I came here seeking employment. I never thought to see you here."

"And now that you have? As I recall, we didn't part under the best of circumstances."

"Oh, you mean about Father?" Falcon shrugged again. "Yes, that angered me for a long time, but you can get over many things in the galleys."

"Don't trust him, my lord," Marco warned.

"I make my own decisions," de Beaumont said. He mused for a few minutes. The Draco de Montfalcon he had known had been a lively youth, his mind quick, his opinions as strongly held as those of his father, Eudes. This was not how he would have expected him to turn out. Still, the galleys *did* have the reputation for turning men into mindless brutes. "Give him his clothes," he said at length.

Marco tossed the bundle of garments at Falcon, who dressed himself without haste. When he was clothed, de Beaumont said: "Come, we'll talk further in my quarters." Falcon followed de Beaumont from the cell, and Marco walked behind him. Falcon walked unsteadily, frequently stumbling against the passage wall. He hoped that he was not making his act too obvious. He was counting his steps, measuring the passage. After all, he *had* wanted to see the inside of this place, though he had not anticipated doing it under such circumstances. Since he could do nothing else, he might as well perform a reconnaissance.

Falcon blinked in the strong sunlight as they emerged into a courtyard. He did a quick scan of the stables and sheds that crowded the open space, orienting himself by the mountain peaks that towered over the battlements.

De Beaumont led him to an outside stairway that led up to a long gallery. It was unlike any castle architecture Falcon was familiar with, and he had to remind himself of the place's checkered history as Roman fort and Christian abbey. De Beaumont entered one of the rooms opening off the gallery, and Falcon followed with Marco at his heels. He was not as weak as he pretended to be, but the short walk and climb had tired him. De Beaumont gestured toward a chest, and Falcon gratefully sat on it.

De Beaumont sat on his cathedra. "Marco, bring us some wine." The Lombard poured wine into goblets and handed one to his master and another to Falcon, then poured some for himself. He eyed the prisoner with bleak hostility tinged with respect and what might have been a superstitious dread.

Falcon sipped at the wine. After the deprivations of recent days, it would go quickly to his head, and he couldn't afford that.

"Tell me of your adventures, Draco," de Beaumont began. "How did you escape the galley? I have heard of your capture after Hattin, and that Valdemar had callously sold you into slavery. How on earth did you gain your freedom?"

"We were shipwrecked on the Greek coast by a storm. Salvagers took off the rowers who hadn't drowned. They sold the heathens, but the Christians were set free. I took service in the Greek emperor's army for a while, but there's no honor in fighting in lines and formations. I killed some men in battle and they said I was ritually impure and couldn't receive the sacraments for two years. I could do without the sacraments, but it was stupid to be called impure for killing the enemies you're ordered to fight, so I left." He took another small swallow of the wine.

"I caught a ship bound for Venice and made my way from there to the South of France. I picked up some brigands to serve me as followers, and we've been picking up a living here and there, fighting in little wars and squabbles over land and cattle."

"A poor existence for such a man as you," de Beaumont said. Falcon merely shrugged. "Aren't you curious about what became of your men?"

"Why?" Falcon said. "They were just hirelings."

"A better quality of hireling than most. Besides the havoc you wrought among my men in the village, they killed ten more at the mouth of the gorge in making their escape. I would not have thought that possible to men on foot and poorly armed."

"I trained them well," Falcon observed.

"Very well, indeed. One thing struck me as curious. All ten heads were cut off and piled neatly near the standing stone."

"That would be Donal's doing," Falcon said.

"And who might Donal be?"

"He's an Irishman in my service. The Irish like to collect heads."

"Admirable. My own men are fond of such sport." The Black Pope fixed him with a cold stare. "Now, Draco, though it is a painful subject, we must address the question of your future. As I see it, that future may be severely limited."

"If it's ransom you want, I'll have to disappoint you. I haven't a sou. No land and no lord. I own only my sword and armor."

"No, I own them now." De Beaumont waved a large, pudgy hand. "No matter, I don't accept ransom, anyway."

"No ransom," Falcon said, screwing his face up into an

expression of incomprehension. "Then what do you fight for?"

"I have my goals, In time, perhaps, you will be privy to my secrets. If you live. That is, after all, the question: Shall I let you live?"

"If you will, I'll serve you faithfully," Falcon said. "I'll take your oath."

"Any oath you take will not be just to me, but to my Master," de Beaumont said.

"Your Master? Who is that?" The hair at Falcon's neck prickled, but he fought to keep his expression one of simple-minded puzzlement.

"That you need not know just yet. I have but one need of you now. Those men of yours, the footmen: They fought better than any I've ever heard of save a few Saracen foot we encountered in Outremer. Was that a result of your training?"

"I'm a good trainer of soldiers," Falcon said. "Those villeins were just common brigands before I forged them into a fighting team. You know how Father was about the common soldiers: Train them well and treat them almost like equals, and they can outfight knights, given the chance." It wrenched Falcon's heart to invoke his father's memory to buy his life from his father's betrayer, but he had no choice. His revenge would come in time.

Marco barked a short, vicious laugh. "Footmen fight like knights? Common scum cannot stand before armored horsemen of good blood!"

"Still," de Beaumont chided, "those 'common filth' accounted for quite a number of your men. And you didn't account for a single man of them."

"My men have seen a good deal of that fine blood you boast of," Falcon said.

"A fluke," Marco blustered. "In the village, it was dark. I don't know what happened at the gorge, but I'll wager those swine caught my men dismounted."

"What good are soldiers who can only fight in good light or from the backs of animals?" Falcon snorted. He knew he was making an eneny, but there was little choice.

"And what kind of knight are you?" Marco shouted. "You make common cause against your kind with base louts and peasants! My lord has said that you are the son of one of the most illustrious chevaliers of the Crusading armies, yet you talk like the leader of—of—" The Lombard searched his limited vocabulary for a suitably contemptuous epithet. "Of *archers!*"

"I'm a knight who has sat at a Turkish bench for years, pulling a Turkish oar and feeling a Turkish whip across his back," Falcon said. "It gives a man a different way of looking at things. I'm a knight who has stood in ranks with Greek foot soldiers and served sword to Pechenegs and the like. I'm still a knight as good as any, but I've learned that there's more to soldiering then lowering your lance and charging at whatever's in front of you. War means killing, and I've learned to kill better than any nobleman who never went East." This last was perfectly true.

"Cease this bickering!" de Beaumont barked. "Marco, if I wish to make use of this man's talents, it is not for you to find fault. Draco, if you would live, you shall not dispute with my chief captain. Is that understood by you both?" He glowered at the two.

"As my lord wishes, of course," said Marco, with poor grace but lowering his head in humility.

"Understood," Falcon said, "if you really intend to take me into your service. Do you?"

"Certainly. I knew your father as a peerless knight. I knew you as a boy who had it in him to surpass the father. I would have such a man as my servant. Marco, when you took the service of myself and our Master, you renounced all your former allegiances—to your former liege, to your class, and to God. I remind you of that oath." The Lombard bowed his head in acquiescence once more.

"Draco," de Beaumont said, "some of my men were found with arrows through them. It was a new kind of arrow—long, and capable of piercing mail. I've never seen such arrows. They were too long for crossbows, and even among the Saracens I never saw long bows that would wreak such havoc. It would be good to have such bowmen among my followers."

"I fear I cannot help you there," Falcon said. "There were two Welshmen in my following, brothers, they were. They had bows such as I've never seen before: great brutes, six feet or more in length, of yew. Given good wood, I think I could have such bows made, but it takes a lifetime to make fine archers, just like knights."

"A pity. Such bowmen could go far to make up for a decided inferiority of numbers." Falcon reflected that whatever madness had overcome de Beaumont, it had not affected his sharp military instincts. The former archbishop turned to Falcon with a benign expression. "Well, Draco, will you take my service?"

"Gladly," Falcon said. Painfully, he shifted himself from the chest he was sitting on and knelt on one knee, his hands folded as if in prayer before him. He had no qualms about taking an oath of fealty to de Beaumont. By the values in which he had been raised, no oath to a kinslayer was binding.

"On both knees, Draco," said de Beaumont mildly.

"Both knees?" said Falcon, nonplussed. "That's not how I learned it. On one knee to my liege, be he captain or king. On both knees only to God."

"By this oath you renounce God, Draco. You take oath not only to me, but to my Master, who is greater than God."

Hardened as he was, these words chilled Falcon to the

bone. His years in the wars in Outremer and in the galleys and in the service of Suleiman had broadened his tolerance far beyond that of any European, but an oath to what must be a Satanic power was nothing to take lightly, albeit insincere. Still, there was no choice. To combat this man's evil, to revenge his father, he would undergo anything, though it destroy his very soul. He lowered his other knee to the floor.

Still standing, de Beaumont took the folded hands between his own. "You will repeat these words after me: 'I, Draco de Montfalcon, do hereby renounce all former oaths.'" Falcon droned the words, and those that followed. "'I do submit myself, body and soul, to the service of the Black Pope, to do his bidding in all things. I renounce my family, my former liege, and my God. Henceforth, I acknowledge neither Christ nor Mohammed, neither Cross nor Crescent, neither Gospel nor Koran. All that was once evil to me I shall find good, if my lord call it so. This I swear, by the Master who rules us all." Inwardly, Falcon told himself that these were just words, but it was not easy. In his time and place, words were everything.

"Rise, Draco," de Beaumont said, beaming. He embraced his new servant warmly, then he turned to Marco. "Marco, this man is now your brother." Without enthusiasm, the Lombard knight embraced Falcon as his master had done.

"And now," de Beaumont said, "I think that supper should be ready in the hall."

Once again, de Beaumont led, followed by Falcon, with Marco in the rear. The Black Pope led them to a huge room, probably once the refectory of the monks who had formerly lived here, possibly also the mess hall of its one-time Roman garrison. Two long tables ran down its center, and at one end was a raised dais which held another table at right angles to the lower ones. De Beaumont strode to the high table and seated Falcon at his left hand. He clapped once, and servitors began bringing in the food and drink.

Falcon studied the men seated at the benches. Except for their monklike black robes, they appeared much like any other pack of knightly feasters. Without their black armor and ominous helms, they were no more fearsome than others. They looked dangerous and deadly, but all knights were expected to. Falcon heard a number of tongues being spoken, but most seemed to favor French, mainly in its southern dialects. He saw a few who had a decidedly Arabic appearance, and one definite Turk. What kind of hellish fraternity had de Beaumont assembled?

The servitors were all men; small, slight of build, and dark. Falcon could not guess for certain their origin. They carried platters of precious metals heaped with meats, cheeses, and loaves. Instead of the usual bread trenchers, the knights were served on rich plate, their wine poured into chalices. Falcon could see that most of the tableware had once graced the altars of the churches.

"You live well here," Falcon observed.

"Our Master rewards his followers in this life rather than the next," de Beaumont said. Their raids had netted them plenty of cattle and sheep and pigs. One rarely saw so much fresh meat except at fall slaughtering time. As with the wine, Falcon forced himself to be moderate, pacing his intake to avoid becoming ill and wasting this opportunity to stock his body's depleted reserves. The food was excellently cooked, most of it in the Eastern fashion, subtly spiced and prepared with delicate sauces. Spices were not usually a part of European cooking, or where they could be afforded, they were used lavishly to kill the taste of preserved or spoiled meats.

Falcon pared a thin slice of cheese, laid it atop a piece of bread, and laid a strip of beef atop that. He bit into it and devoured it slowly, in small bites. De Beaumont was watching him closely. "You have a care for your health," he noted.

"No sense gorging and puking," Falcon said.

"You know, Draco, I really don't believe you're quite as dull as you make yourself out to be." That was unfortunate, but he hadn't expected de Beaumont to accept his entire act.

"Why are there no women here?" Falcon asked.

"My men need no women," de Beaumont said.

"Why? Are they all monks, or eunuchs?"

"No," chuckled de Beaumont. "Far from it." Feeling like a fly in a spiderweb, Falcon returned his attention to his food.

SEVEN

TWO knights faced Falcon. Both wore the head-covering helms and full mail. All three men carried the long, black featureless shields. Falcon wore his customary mailshirt and conical helmet. Behind its noseguard, his eyes glittered dangerously. The two knights stood crouched behind their shields, far enough apart to allow each other room to wield their weapons.

Suddenly, Falcon leaped at the man on his right. The knight swung an overhand blow aimed to split Falcon's helm and automatically raised his own shield against a counterblow. Falcon dodged the sword and hooked the left edge of his shield behind that of his opponent. With a hard jerk, he used the leverage of the man's own shield against him, spinning the knight around. The edge of Falcon's dull practice sword slammed into the man's back over the kidney. With a knee in the knight's buttocks, Falcon sent him tumbling against the other man, who had been trying to maneuver himself around his companion for a clear blow at Falcon. The falling man caused the other to stumble back slightly, moving his arms apart to keep his balance. The lapse of defense was brief, but it was all Falcon needed. He was inside the man's guard in an instant, bringing the sword down against the heavy helm in a blow that sent the man sprawling. There were murmurs of approval from the watching knights.

"Very pretty, Draco," said de Beaumont. The Black Pope eyed his latest recruit with approval. In a very few days, Draco had recovered his full strength, and he moved under the weight of his arms as if dressed in hose and jerkin. Eudes had been like that, but where had his son learned to fight with such fluid grace and precision? There was never a waste motion, and he seldom needed more than a single blow to deal with an opponent. Most knights swung their swords with enough power to split a man from brow to crotch, and the effort showed. Draco's blows seemed to lack force, yet they were blindingly swift and landed with shattering force. What a puzzle the man was.

"They could fight better without those iron masks," Falcon said.

"I've told you before, Draco, that no outsider may ever see the faces of my men. It is forbidden by our Master."

"And," Falcon continued, "they'd do better without those mail hose. Men on foot have no use for them. They're heavy and cumbersome. A man who manages his shield properly can protect his legs well enough without them, and he'll move more freely."

"Why should knights need to excel at foot fighting?" Marco demanded. "The common rabble can handle that." In most armies, the footmen had no purpose except to be slaughtered for the knights' sport.

"I can see you've never served in Palestine," Falcon said. "The horses die quickly over there, and the Saracen breed are too small for armored men. In bad seasons, I've fought whole campaigns when there weren't ten good warhorses in the entire army."

"Draco's right about that," de Beaumont. "We all had to learn to be foot soldiers in the East."

"And then, there are castles," Draco said. "You can't take a castle from horseback."

"Castles!" Marco snorted. "It's always the same: the knights go up the ladders or cross from siege towers. Once you're in, there's never more than an hour or two of fighting before the surrender. The common soldiers have no armor and are all killed. If you meet another knight, then it's man to man and the stronger wins with no need of these juggler's tricks."

"I fear that Marco is a warrior of the old school," de Beaumont said.

"That may have been true of the old castles," Falcon said. "They were just a stockade around a keep. But the wars in the East have changed all that. The new ones, like Richard Plantaganet's Chateau Gaillard, can take days of foot fighting from one strongpoint to another. An army of nothing but heavy cavalry is no good anymore. You need disciplined foot and engineers as well. And the knights have to know something besides how to spear other horsemen." Marco looked unconvinced.

"There's much in what you say," de Beaumont said. "But, Draco, when you ride out of here on my business, you must wear the great helm like the others."

"As my lord wishes," Falcon said. Since he had no intention of fighting anybody for de Beaumont, the promise cost him nothing.

It was his first day as training master to de Beaumont. The knights were no better and no worse than most. The two Arabs and the Turk were much more apt at Falcon's style of combat than the Westerners. Those who had been in the East were more at home on foot than others, but they didn't fight efficiently that way. He had not yet tested their quality from horseback, but he knew that they would be competent. No one of knightly rank survived to young manhood if he was not.

From what he had seen of the men, they were oddly ordinary, except for their occasional exotic oaths. He had yet to discover the source of their extraordinary ferocity and seeming madness when raiding. He thought of the drug-taking habits of the Assassins. Were these men similarly intoxicated before being sent out?

De Beaumont had told him little. He was clearly still under suspicion, and he could not afford to pry too deeply. Each evening, the knights went to perform some ceremony behind the bolted doors of the old chapel. At these times, Falcon was locked in the great hall along with the servants and a few of the other knights who were on probationary status. While thus incarcerated, Falcon had tried to talk to the servants, but the men seemed mute.

He tried not to brood upon what had become of his men. Wulf, he knew, would do all within his power to win Falcon's freedom. The others? They were good men, hand-picked, but they had served him only a short time. Also, they had good reason to judge that he had failed them. They had taken his oath, but his position was more that of paymaster than feudal lord.

There came a day when most of the knights rode out on a foray into the lowlands. Supplies were running low. All the night before, the knights had spent in the chapel, from which Falcon was still barred. When they emerged in the morning, they were transformed. Faces were flushed, eyes started and gazed about restlessly, men wore fierce, teeth-baring grins that disappeared only when they donned the face-hiding helms. They rode out, spurring their mounts cruelly and screaming like a pack of lunatics.

Falcon watched them go with an eye to his chances for

escape. Those were still slim. Nearly a third of the knights had stayed behind. These had not participated in the night's ceremonies and were at least as sane as usual, and the regular guard was mounted upon the walls. The battlements were no great barrier. A dark night and an easily obtained piece of rope were all he needed to get away. The sentries could be dealt with. Falcon could move as silently as any Assassin when he needed to, and he was handy with the dagger and the bowstring noose.

His problem was more complicated. He needed not only to escape, but to kill de Beaumont first. Even that was no major obstacle, but, before killing him, Falcon had to have some answers from the man. He knew de Beaumont to be a strong man of great personal courage. The questioning would take a long time, and de Beaumont would make a great deal of noise before surrendering his secrets.

Time was the crucial factor. Even taking into consideration the snail-like speed of a feudal hosting, it could not be much longer before the lowland army appeared in the mountain valley to clean out the Black Pope's castle and, incidentally, Goatsfoot and all the other villages hereabout. Falcon was adamant: He would not leave these mountains alive without accomplishing his revenge and finding out the truth about his father.

These dark thoughts went through his mind as he stood in the courtyard, staring at the disappearing horsemen while the great gates slowly closed. Above him, de Beaumont appeared on the gallery, dressed as always in his black robes.

"Draco, come and join me in my chamber."

"Yes, my lord." He felt the beginnings of a mild excitement. The Black Pope had not invited him for a private audience before.

In the room, Falcon's eyes required a few moments to adjust to the dimness. De Beaumont gestured toward the pitcher and cups on the sideboard, and Falcon poured cups full of the deep-red liquid and handed one to de Beaumont. Falcon sipped at his own. His eyes strayed to his great sword Nemesis, which hung upon the wall. His hands itched to grasp its long, two-handed grip. If only it were simply a matter of killing de Beaumont. God damn Gunther Valdemar! he thought furiously. Were it not for the German knight's cryptic words about his father, he could simply accomplish his revenge and carve his way out of this place.

"A remarkable weapon," de Beaumont observed, following Falcon's gaze. "Where did you come by it?"

"I took it from a Saracen I killed, along with the helmet and armor."

"That's uncommon. I don't think I've ever seen a Saracen as big as you, yet the helmet and the mail fit you perfectly." De Beaumont's questions were probing, although his tone was one of light inconsequential conversation.

"That was a stroke of luck," Falcon said. "He was a great big bugger of a Circassian. They look almost like us, you know. Some have light hair and blue eyes. This one did."

"Ah, a Circassian. That would explain it," de Beaumont mused. "The sword, now, that's a truly marvelous weapon. Except for a few executioner's swords, I've never seen a scimitar so large, made to wield two-handed. And it's a true Damascus blade."

"I suppose it is," Falcon said offhandedly. "It has that look—as if the blade were made of watered silk." He could contemplate the blade's perfect polish and mottled coloring for hours. Even speaking of Nemesis made him hunger to have her belted to his side once more. "It's sharper and harder than any other sword I've ever handled. It took a bit of getting used to—the curve of the blade and using it two-handed without a shield. But once you've the knack, it's a better design than a straight sword."

"When I first saw it," de Beaumont said, "I knew that it reminded me of something. Last night, I remembered what it was." From his table, he picked up a small book. "This is something I bought in the East. Do you read Arabic?"

"No," Falcon lied. "I can't read anything."

"Well, this is called *Tales from the Days of Harun al-Rashid*." Harun al-Rashid, Falcon knew, was the greatest of the caliphs of Baghdad. Moslems looked back to his reign as a golden age, just as Christendom did to the reign of his contemporary, Charlemagne.

"What had stuck in my memory," de Beaumont went on, "was a passage in a story called 'The Fortunes of Abu the Thief.' Among this enterprising gentleman's acquisitions was a sword which he purloined from a cave inhabited by a giant. Here is how the sword is described." De Beaumont's voice took on his story-telling mode.

"In the time of King Solomon, there lived a swordmaker named Seth, son of Aaron, and the king sent to him, ordering that a sword be made for him which was to surpass all other blades. It was to be used for the righting of wrongs, and for the execution of the king's judgment against wrongdoers. Seth lavished all his skill upon this sword, and this was its form: Its blade was longer than others, and curved like the crescent moon. Its hilt and pommel were likewise curved as the crescent of the moon, and from these three crescents was derived the name of the sword, which was called Three Moons. It was stolen from the tomb of Solomon by a genie who wished for revenge because the king had sealed him and all his kind in bottles, from which this genie had been freed by an ignorant peasant. The sword was given to the giant by the genie in payment of a wager, but neither of these unholy creatures could use it because of the spell of righteousness placed upon it by King Solomon. It was this selfsame sword which Abu beheld upon the wall of the giant's cave." De Beaumont put the book down. Falcon knew the story. Suleiman had told him the tale, and the young Draco had been awestruck, but Suleiman was of the opinion that the sword was no more than two hundred years old. It was inevitable, he had explained, that anything of fabulous quality, be it weapon or building or hero's deeds, quickly acquired a body of spurious legend in the common mind.

"In the margin, here," de Beaumont went on, "is a comment, written recently in a different hand. It says: 'The great sword called Three Moons was until recently in the possession of the scholar and magistrate Suleiman the Wise. Suleiman is believed to have died at the siege of Acre, and he may have been among the prisoners treacherously slaughtered by Al Ric. No man can now say where Three Moons resides.' " De Beaumont closed the book. Al Ric was the Saracen name for Richard Lion-Heart of England. "Just think, Draco—this may be that legendary sword. It certainly answers to the description here."

"Three Moons is a pretty name. I'd named her Breadwinner because I make my living with her," Draco lied, afraid that if he gave his sword's real name, Nemesis, de Beaumont would realize that his loyalty was a sham, and his desire for the revenge of his father's death was very much alive. Behind his careless pose, he was in turmoil. De Beaumont knew Suleiman's name! Did he know more, or was this just a fantastic coincidence?

"Breadwinner!" De Beaumont threw back his head and roared with laughter. "Leave it to a Western knight to make something prosaic out of the fabulous!" He subsided into a series of chuckles that made his chins and belly quiver like a plate of jellied eels. When he was once more under control he went on. "Well, Draco, I think I can trust you now, and I can see that you're afire to have the blade back. Go and belt it on."

Falcon fairly darted to the wall. With the precious weapon belted to his side, he felt whole for the first time in many days. "Thank you, my lord," he said. "You won't regret your confidence." *Not just yet, anyway, you treacherous bastard,* he thought.

"I'm sure of that. Now, to more important matters. Draco, how much do you know of the Templars?"

"The Templars?" Falcon said guardedly. "Not much, of late. I saw the last of their guard fall around the Beauséant at Hattin, just before I made my escape with the remnants of Raymond of Tripoli's forces." The Beauséant was the Templars' famous standard, lost along with the True Cross at the disastrous battle. "Nothing much since then. I've heard that they've rebuilt their strength and they're still as rich as ever." The famous Crusading order possessed the strongest castles in the world, and as a result many princes and nobles committed their treasures to their care. The Templars had become a veritable banking institution, especially in France.

"Did you know that they have a policy of recruiting men who have been excommunicated?"

"Yes, but they've always done that, haven't they? It's supposed to give them the chance to reenter the good graces of Christendom." He saw de Beaumont make a peculiar gesture at the word.

"So it was, once. Now, they are a different order, with different goals. I have frequent dealings with the Templars. Does that surprise you, Draco?"

"Nothing you do surprises me, my lord."

"That's good, Draco." De Beaumont leaned back in his cathedra and laced his fingers across his capacious paunch. "In many ways, the new Temple resembles my own Black Army, but they are not prepared to go as far as I have. They've chosen to remain within the confines of

Christendom, which I have rejected utterly. This is because they value their wealth too highly, and have no true confidence in our Master. Cowards!" He snorted. "If they possessed true faith, with their numbers and treasure, we could bring down the Throne of St. Peter and the outdated Church of Christ in a fortnight. I am surrounded by cowards and fools, Draco. My men are brave, but like most they are stupid. The leaders of the Temple are cunning, but they lack spine. I wish I had more men like you, Draco—brave and resourceful and far more clever than you let on."

"I am flattered, my lord."

"Yes, I know you're no dullard. But I don't hold your little deception against you. You would truly be a fool if you exposed your strongest merits before knowing your situation, but don't you think it's time we ceased these little games between us?"

"As you say, my lord." Falcon was ready to make this concession. If de Beaumont thought that he had won something by the admission, he might not go looking for more secrets. "Since you honor me with your trust now, may I ask a question that has been puzzling me?"

"Very well. Ask."

"Just who or what *is* our Master?"

"Now, now, Draco," de Beaumont said, waggling an admonitory finger, as if to a child, "you aren't quite ready for *that* just yet. The final mysteries will be made clear to you in time. I'm pleased with your progress so far, but some things must be absorbed gradually, even by the wisest man."

Idly, de Beaumont took the book from the table. Fishing a key from somewhere inside his robes, he went to a chest and unlocked it. As he placed the book inside, Falcon caught a glimpse of stacks of books and parchments, then the lid was shut again. He longed for a leisurely look at those documents, but how? De Beaumont seemed never to leave the fortress.

"Another thing, my lord, if you don't mind."

"Yes?" de Beaumont said, reseating himself and picking up his cup.

"Those village people. Your men have left them untouched. Considering what they do in the low country, I'm surprised to find anything alive nearby."

"Oh, them," de Beaumont said. "You need not concern yourself. We need laborers occasionally, and they have nothing worth taking, as you must have seen for yourself. They're not Christians, anyway. Besides . . ." De Beaumont leaned back, rolling his cup between his palms, a faraway look in his eyes. "I have—plans—for them all."

Falcon gazed at the new helm, hefting it in both hands. It was black, like the others, with narrow eye slits and tiny breathing holes. With its slanting eye slits and angular planes it looked sinister, evil. An artisan among the servants had crafted it at de Beaumont's orders for Falcon. The crest disturbed him. Like the rest it was black, made of leather boiled in wax and molded into shape in the form of the head and arching neck of a falcon, its beak gaping savagely. From the sides of the helm sprang a pair of black wings made of thick, painted parchment, and they towered above the helm more than a foot. Below the wings were stretched the legs and talons of the bird, and these were genuine falcon's legs, with some feathers still sprouting from them.

When he had returned from the East and changed his name to Falcon, Draco had chosen the bird of prey as his shield device. It depicted, against a silver field, a black falcon, its wings spread, clutching in its talons bolts of blue lightning. Had de Beaumont somehow learned of this? Was this helm his way of telling Falcon that he knew? Or was it just another coincidence? Falcon was too experienced a campaigner to have any trust in coincidence.

The thing was heavy, nine or ten pounds. Inside, it was thickly padded with straw-stuffed leather. Falcon set the helm on the ground and drew his hood of mail over his head. He pulled the iron-mesh veil across his face and tied it to the lace that dangled at his temple. The veil, called an aventail, covered the lower part of his nose, so that only his eyes showed. His fine hauberk fell to just below his knees, and it had tightly fitted sleeves to the wrist. The hood, or coif, covered head, face, and throat. Thus accoutered, he needed only to clap on his conical helmet and pull on his thick, spike-studded leather gauntlets to be fully armored for battle. That was in normal times. Now he picked up the heavy helm and placed it atop his mailed head.

It took a firm shove with both hands to force the iron barrel helm down over the coif. The thick padding held it firmly, without the necessity of a chinstrap. He shook his head a few times to assure himself of its firm seating. Unused to its weight, easily five or six times that of his helmet, he felt the strain in his neck muscles. The field of vision was wider than he had thought, because the narrow eye slits were close to the eyes. Still, peripheral vision was severely limited, and looking down was impossible. At rest, he had no trouble breathing, but he knew that prolonged exertion would quickly turn the air stale inside, and that the tiny air holes provided inadequate ventilation. They had to be small, because the only real advantage of the barrel helm was that it provided a solid, curved or slanted surface that would cause a lance point to slip off harmlessly. If they were too large, the point would catch and the helm would be torn from the wearer's head and he would be lucky to escape a broken neck.

In Falcon's opinion, it was an entirely unsatisfactory

piece of military equipment and a decided step in the wrong direction. Besides its other faults, it was hot. The padding allowed no heat to escape, and a hot sun would merely add to the wearer's woes. He had seen such helms worn in his last years in Palestine, and had seen riders reel in the saddle and fall dead in the midst of battle without taking a wound. In the broiling Eastern sun, it was often a race between suffocation and heat stroke to see which would kill a man first.

Falcon looked about the courtyard. The open space was crowded with men, most talking or engaged in some activity, but only muffled sounds came to his ears. As a crowning inefficiency, the barrel helm rendered the wearer nearly deaf.

Most knights considered hearing superfluous. The average European knight fought on his own, as a little mobile fortress, protected by his armor and the height and weight of his horse. All he required of a leader was to point him in the right direction and provide him with an enemy. After that, his personal courage, strength, and honor were all that mattered. Falcon had never tolerated that kind of independence among his own men. Each had to be able to hear orders and respond to them instantly, even in the heat of battle. Even that valiant lunkhead Ruy Ortiz, Falcon's master of horse, had had to learn that hard lesson, though it had taken many ferocious tongue-lashings, followed by soothing appeasements of honor, to teach him to respond to command.

Falcon sighed. Time to try this bucket out. He took his horse's reins from one of the swarthy servants and vaulted lightly into the saddle, without touching his stirrups. This was something Eudes had always insisted upon, as a knight had to be able to remount swiftly if he was unhorsed in battle. The watchers applauded the feat, though Falcon could not hear them. He took his lance from the servant.

Falcon took the long black shield which was hung from the pommel of his saddle. It was triangular in shape, curved to give the sides of the body some protection. Falcon preferred the kite shield, which had a rounded top, but this was cut straight across the top, in the new fashion. The protection of the barrel helm obviated the necessity of extra protection. Falcon had always considered proper shield-handling of more use than reliance on armor, but there was no fighting military fashion.

At the far end of the courtyard a quintain had been set up. This simple mechanism consisted of an upright post with a pivoted beam set atop it. On one end of the beam was a small shield, at the other a heavy sandbag. Inevitably, the feel of the lance and the sight of the quintain brought back to him his boyhood and the long days of his tutelage under Odo FitzRoy, friend and betrayer of his father. His vengeance upon FitzRoy was the event he most looked forward to. He had loved Odo, and his hatred was consequently the greater.

Spurring his horse to a swift canter, he bore down upon the quintain. His lance caught the shield squarely in the center, and he automatically ducked as the sandbag whizzed through the space where his head had been. In his youth, he had been knocked sprawling more times than he could count. The training was inescapable for a horseman, and even now Falcon tilted at the quintain every day of his life when he was in garrison.

"Bravo, Draco," shouted de Beaumont. The Black Pope was observing from the gallery. Falcon trotted over to him and removed his helm. "Nicely timed, as always," de Beaumont continued. "I see you haven't forgotten the training you took under Eudes and Odo. How do you like the new helm?"

"It's a waste of good iron," Falcon said. "You could make three good casques out of this one."

De Beaumont roared with laughter. "You have no true

appreciation of terror, Draco. How many times did we see the Saracens break and run when faced with a line of those inhuman masks?"

"They learned," Falcon answered. "And they learned damned quickly, at that, as I'm sure you well remember."

"That they did, my boy, that they did. But it's the quick victory that counts, don't you agree?"

"Yes, my lord," Falcon said, nodding and gritting his teeth.

"Don't you think the crest is fitting?" de Beaumont said, with a cherubic smile.

"It's just a bird," Falcon said with a shrug.

"Not just a bird, but a falcon. After all, you're a de Montfalcon. The creature's in your very name. A bird of prey, noblest of the hunting fowl. Most fitting, I would say."

"As you say, my lord, most fitting." This he said with the deepest conviction.

EIGHT

"**A**T least he's alive," Donal said. From an over-hanging crag, he and Wulf observed Falcon's quintain practice in the courtyard. They lay on their bellies, their faces screened against detection by scrubby bushes which they had cut below. The protection was probably unnecessary, because the sentries on the walls below were relieving the boredom of their duties by watching the action in the courtyard. Even so, Donal and Wulf were not the kind of men who took chances unnecessarily.

"Look at him!" Wulf said. "Enough iron on his head to equip a small army. At least he has Nemesis back."

"That must have taken some doing," the Irishman said. "How do you suppose he did it?"

"Leave it to my lord to get thrown into a dungeon and come out a trusted lieutenant. It isn't the first time."

"He's a rare one, our master. Shall we bring him out of there? We could wait until nightfall. With some ropes and grapples and a little quick ax and dagger work, we could have him free in minutes and be back in the lowland by sunrise."

"No, I think not," Wulf said. "Right now, I'd say he's

exactly where he wants to be. He always said that there's no better place to be than sitting at your enemy's table and drinking his ale." They crawled back until they were out of sight and seated themselves on the rocks. "He won't leave these mountains until he's had his vengeance on that fat priest. We're his men and we have to help him accomplish it."

"Damned inconvenient place for it," Donal said. He picked up a rock and threw it at a lizard, scoring a hit. "Dirt-poor, no food save what'll keep a man barely alive, no towns and no taverns. It's no life for a soldier."

"Plenty of women, though," Wulf said, grinning. "Have you gone without since we've been here?"

"That I've not," said the Irishman. Despite his hideous scars, Donal was a notorious ladies' man. "The women hereabout know a good man when they see one." He wore a complacent smile. These inbred valleys valued any infusion of new blood, and the two had been the recipients of some unexpected hospitality. Then the Irishman turned serious. "What do you think became of Simon? Think he found the army and they're headed this way?"

"It's too early to start worrying," Wulf said. "They're only three men. They have to travel carefully to get to the men with our message. They may already be there, but even an army like ours moves slowly. They'll have to dicker with every lord whose land they pass through and pay tolls or fight their way through. It takes time."

"Time," Donal mused. "Do we have all that much of it?"

They had been hiding out among the mountain villages for weeks. The people had concealed them willingly, but the mountain villagers were slow to realize just how great was their danger. The black riders were an enigma, and the lowlands were a world away. These people were set firmly in their ways and could not respond readily to sudden change.

"Think the Old Woman's been having any luck?" Donal asked. They had come to hold Lilitha in high esteem. She was forceful and intelligent and, though neither would admit it, they were a little afraid of her. After all, the woman was a witch, and who knew what unearthly powers she might have? In any case, she was an ally, and she had smoothed their way among the mountain villagers. Besides that, she was beautiful and regal, and they were men whose upbringing conditioned them to respond to these qualities. It mattered little that she was only a village headwoman; she was queenly in manner and bearing, and that was enough for them.

"I hope so," Wulf said. "I don't know how much good it will do, though. Can you really make fighting men out of these sheep?"

"They're not sheep," Donal protested. "Mountaineers are tough, they have to be. They just aren't used to fighting. Some of them are pretty good with the sling."

"Useless against men in armor," Wulf said. "Especially when they wear those bucket helms."

"Maybe we could teach them to aim at the horses' heads," Donal hazarded.

"That's an idea. Spears might be better. With long pikes, standing shoulder to shoulder, they might be able to hold off the first charge, then swamp the knights with numbers. The Scots fight that way."

"Haven't you looked at the trees hereabout?" Donal said. "They're stunted and gnarled. Even the biggest ones are too twisted to make good spear shafts with."

"I'd forgotten that," Wulf said, chunking a rock at nothing in particular. Falcon would know what to do. Wulf just wasn't used to doing this kind of planning. Given the cooperation of the villagers and a little time, his master could weld them into a fighting force that could give any army in Christendom a good drubbing. No sense wishing for the impossible. He would just have to work with what he had.

"Are these all you could get?" Wulf asked, dismayed.

"They'll have to do," Lilitha said.

"Do what?" Donal asked disgustedly. Before them stood a band of village men, no more than thirty of them. Most were young, little more than boys, dressed in rough homespun, and not a weapon among them except for slings and staffs.

"Here, you," Donal said, indicating a squat youth who had a sling wrapped around his brow. "Let's see what you can do with that." The boy unwound the sling and took a stone from the pouch at his waist. He placed the stone in the sling's pouch and swung it idly.

"What do you want him to sling it at?" Lilitha asked.

"That flower over there," Wulf said, pointing at a small yellow bloom that reared its head against a rock about fifty paces away.

"That's a long cast, for a slinger," Donal said. The woman pointed to the flower and said something in the mountain tongue. The boy fixed his eye on the target and regarded it balefully, the stone swinging at his side. In one motion, he brought the sling up and around his head and sent the stone whizzing faster than thought toward the mark. The observers saw the petals scatter as the stone shattered against the larger rock.

"Not bad, for a slinger," said Donal, scratching his scrubby beard.

"David couldn't have done better," Wulf said.

"Who?" Lilitha asked.

"A famous slinger," Wulf said. "Killed a giant once, a long time ago. Let's see the others." The rest proved to be equally handy with their slings. Their staff work was likewise skillful, but Wulf and Donal knew that it would be

105

futile against armored warriors, whether or not they were mounted.

"They've got spirit," Wulf said, when all had been tested, "but spirit's not enough. We've got to have better weaponry than this." He scanned the terrain. It was typical mountain land; craggy and cut up into narrow valleys, with little level land. "You know, Donal, the master has always said that a good understanding of the land is worth a thousand soldiers on your side. What do you make of this?" A sweep of his arm took in the entire vista.

"Bad for horseback fighting," Donal said. "No flat ground for mounting a charge. Lots of little streams—that makes retreat and pursuit slow. It's almost as bad for foot fighters, though. Little brush and no big trees for cover. Stony ground that's hard to run on. Do you see anything else?"

"There are plenty of overhanging crags," Wulf said. "Those are good places for bowmen or slingers to make ambushes."

"Too bad we don't have any archers," Donal commented.

Wulf contemplated his little "army." "And we're to go up against those fiends with the likes of these."

"They're willing!" Lilitha scolded. "How much have you done since your master was taken?" She drew herself up to her full five or so feet and glared up at the two big men. "These may not be many, and they may not be skilled compared to you, but they are brave men who want to fight the black riders! I've gone out and found men willing to fight. What have you two done except worry and fret since Falcon was taken?" Her bright black eyes glared in scorn at the two.

"Easy, lady," Wulf said. "We speak no ill of you or them. It's just our fashion, as seasoned warriors."

"That's it, you see," Donal said, his palms outward in a

placating manner. "When you're a training sergeant, you always make a great show of how contemptible the new men are. It's traditional and it's good for them."

"Yes, my lady," Wulf said. "I'm sure they're fine lads and will make good warriors, but it doesn't pay to let them know that too soon."

Lilitha looked from one man to the other. She wasn't sure how far to trust them. It was clear that they were loyal to Falcon, but how competent were they? They lacked their master's capabilities, but they seemed to be doing their best. Should she entrust her people's lives to these two? A word from her and these "recruits" would be hotfooting it back to their villages. But should she? For some reason, she had found herself believing Falcon's words about the malevolence of the black riders, and about the danger from the lowlanders. Was she right in this? Or was she merely responding to her carnal yearnings for the big man's rangy body? Her mother and grandmother had drilled into her that it was inexcusable for an Old Woman to make decisions on the basis of her fleshly urges. "Very well," she said. "What do you want them to do now?"

For the rest of the day, the two soldiers had the men practice their slinging, both individually and in unison on command. This last was something new to them, but they responded to the novel discipline well. In fact, their aptitude gave Wulf and Donal much food for thought.

"Lord, Donal," Wulf said at the end of the day, "if a man had the time and a good pay chest, he could make a real army out of these mountain people."

"I told you mountaineers are tough," Donal said. "Didn't I tell you that? The Scots from the highlands are like these men. So are the Basques from Spain. I saw a band of Basque soldiers once, in Greece." The Irishman shook his head in remembered wonder. "All they were armed with were short swords and javelins, but they were so fearsome that the Greek emperor's army would march a hundred leagues out of their way to avoid them. It's the spirit that counts, Wulf. That's why we Irish are the greatest fighters the world's ever seen, you know; we've got the right spirit."

"No doubt," Wulf said. He knew that Donal was about to embark upon one of his interminable tales of Cuchulain or Finn or one of the other Irish heroes. This was an old game between them. In time, Wulf would respond with a tale of Beowulf or Alfred or one of the other Saxon heroes. A good deal of time could be passed in this fashion, he knew. Time. How much did they have left?

Falcon took his great helm off, and a cloud of steam poured from its interior. He took long gulps of air as he untied his aventail and lowered his coif. He had been working the men all day. It was difficult work, because his instinct was to drill them into a state of perfection, but he did not want to make them truly effective soldiers according to his own standards. That was the hard part: to look as if he were whipping this force to a peak of fighting capability, while in truth leaving them just the same pack of aristocratic fools that he'd found. He had to please de Beaumont in order to stay alive, but he wished to go no farther than that.

At least, de Beaumont's force consisted entirely of heavy cavalry. Since the fall of Rome in the West, this had been the most important battle arm, but the wars in the East had taught Falcon and a few other Western leaders the importance of support from the other arms—the usually despised spearmen and bowmen who fought dismounted. Falcon knew that the mounted arm was mainly useful for the first smashing charge and for the pursuit of the broken enemy once they had fallen back. It was essential to keep a broken enemy running and prevent them from making a stand or forming a counterattack. For these purposes, horsemen were indispensable, but the aristocratic horsemen inevitably had a grossly inflated opinion of their own military value. For the nonce, he was content to leave these men with that comforting misconception. He was already regretting his words to Marco and de Beaumont during his first days here. He shouldn't have made such a point of the importance of foot fighting. Marco was unteachable, but already de Beaumont was urging him to drill the men in dismounted combat. The best tactic had proved to be a delaying action: He'd insisted that the men needed to be brought to the highest efficiency in mounted fighting before adding any refinements.

He pondered the hated iron bucket in his hands. That, at least, was a point in his favor. As long as de Beaumont insisted upon his men's wearing the things, they couldn't fight with true efficiency. Falcon knew just how to take advantage of the limitations they imposed on hearing and sight. He smiled grimly at the thought of what experts like his Welsh bowmen and his Genoese crossbowmen could accomplish against these mounted demons. Their horses and mail were futile against the powerful missile weapons of such men.

"Draco, come here!" De Beaumont's peremptory tones shook Falcon from his vengeful reverie. He trotted his horse to where the former prelate was standing. "My lord?" Falcon queried.

"The men will be returning soon from their raid into the low country. I think it may be time for you to join us in our services. Once you've done that, you'll be ready to take part in our raids. I know that an old soldier like you must be champing at the bit, having to stay here while the others go out and have all the sport."

"It's been tedious, my lord," Falcon said.

"Well, soon you'll be one of us in full, Draco." De Beaumont wore a chilling smile.

"It's my fondest wish, my lord," Falcon said.

Later in the day, just before sunset, the riders returned. Before them they drove a sizable herd of livestock, and their pack animals carried bulging bundles of loot. Most interesting to Falcon, though, were the prisoners: three young men, all exceptionally handsome. When Marco rode through the gate, de Beaumont went immediately to meet him. Removing his helm and tossing it to a servant, Marco gave his report.

"Best day's work we've had in a long time, my lord. We caught a village at fair time. We're loaded down with merchants' goods: cloth, spices, wines, plenty of preserved meats and fish and fruit. If we'd had enough beasts, we could've had provisions for a year."

"Excellent," de Beaumont said. Falcon stood behind the Black Pope to hear Marco's report. "Did you let any escape?"

"None, my lord. We surrounded the village at dawn and came charging in before most were awake. I left half the men in the fields around the village while the rest scoured the streets. It took us until midday to kill them all." Marco laughed heartily. "There was a troupe of tumblers there for the fair. They gave us some rare sport with their ducking and dodging before we skewered them all. Most of the villagers tried to take refuge in the church, the way they always do. They were packed in there so tightly they couldn't even fall as we worked our way through them with axes."

"Very good, Marco," de Beaumont said. He turned to Falcon. "Fine work, don't you think, Draco?"

"Why not spare some of the villagers as porters?" Falcon asked. "That way you could have brought all the goods back here instead of having to leave so much."

Marco smiled insolently. "Wait until you ride with us. You won't be able to stop killing until the last victim's dead. It was as much as I could do to keep these three alive." He waved toward the three young men who knelt in the courtyard, chained neck to neck. They wore the blank expressions of men shocked to numbness by what they had been through. De Beaumont walked over to the dispirited little group. One, a youth of no more than sixteen, looked up. The sight of de Beaumont's ecclesiastical garments brought a look of faint hope to the boy's face. De Beaumont stroked the beardless cheek, then pinched it gently, as if to test the smooth skin's resiliency. "There, my pretty," he murmured, "you'll do nicely."

"What are these three for?" Falcon asked.

De Beaumont, still fondling the boy's cheek, turned his beaming face toward Falcon. "They're for tonight," he said. "You'll see, then."

It was near midnight when the servant summoned Falcon from his quarters. He had spent the time since supper steeling himself for what was to come. At supper he had drunk no wine, as it was imperative that he keep a clear head. Whatever hellish rite he was to participate in, he was determined to go through with it. Only thus could he win de Beaumont's full trust. He would let nothing on earth, or in heaven or hell, cheat him of his vengeance. Whatever de Beaumont asked of him, he would do, though it cost him his soul. Keeping his life was all that counted, for only by staying alive could he kill de Beaumont and track down the others and find the truth about his father.

In any case, he had ceased giving overmuch thought to his soul's salvation many years ago. He had lived through too much, seen too much evil too young, much of it committed by the very men he had looked to for religious guidance.

The servant led him to the chapel, where de Beaumont was waiting for him. "The rest are inside, Draco. Come join us and become one of the brethren."

Falcon stooped to enter the low doorway. The room

was large, nearly as big as the hall, and lit garishly by torches set in sconces around the walls. The air was thick with smoke, for the windows were few and narrow. There was no furniture that he could discern, but he could make out an odd shape at the far end of the room. De Beaumont guided him through the chapel, and the men parted to let them through. Their faces were flushed with anticipation, wearing smiles that were almost snarls.

At the far end of the room was an altar. There was no mistaking it, or its intended purpose. It was of stone, and around its sides were a number of bronze rings. It was covered with a black, pitchlike substance. The walls behind and to the sides were spattered with it almost to the ceiling. The smell of dried blood hung thick in the air, competing with the smoke. If de Beaumont had been hoping for a change of expression from Falcon, he was disappointed. Draco Falcon had had a long and intimate acquaintance with blood.

Behind the altar was a sculptured figure. It was so blood-spattered that the details were difficult to make out in the flickering, smoke-dimmed light. The thing was in human shape, a little larger than life-size. It sat crosslegged on a pedestal, arms spread slightly to the sides. Its torso and arms were human, but the head was that of a goat with spiraling horns. Between the horns was a gilt pentagram, and Falcon thought he could detect something Egyptian in the treatment of the head. The legs were likewise goatlike, and from between the spread thighs sprang a long phallus, thin and pointed like a goat's.

"Our Master," de Beaumont intoned. "Baphomet."

Falcon had heard the name before, and he had seen such a goat-headed image, somewhat different in detail, but he said nothing of this. De Beaumont turned to his men and spread his arms wide. "Tonight," he said, opening his arms wide as if embracing the throng, "we are assembled to worship our Master. Once again, we, his people, have been rewarded for our faithfulness. Our Master has given us the abundance of our enemies, and we have given him their blood!" At this, the gathered knights set up a truly demented howling. Falcon could see several large goblets being passed from hand to hand among them. Each knight took a swig from a goblet as he received it, then passed it to the next.

"Now, we share our holy sacrament in token of our union with each other and with Baphomet!" De Beaumont sat himself in a throne to one side of the altar, and he beckoned to Falcon to come stand beside him. A knight brought de Beaumont one of the goblets. The Black Pope took a deep swallow. He handed the cup to Falcon. "Finish it."

Falcon looked into the vessel. The liquid was red but transparent. In the bottom he could see grainy black dregs. De Beaumont never took his eyes off Falcon as he raised the cup. With one swallow, he drained it, gagging slightly on the bitter taste. Whatever the drug was, it had been mixed with wine. He had no idea what the drug might be, but he knew that his tolerance was high. Suleiman had made him take many drugs in small amounts at intervals, in order to build up a resistance to them. The likelihood was good that the brew would not affect him as it would the others.

The men began a chant, wordless and hypnotic. Falcon felt himself beginning to respond to it, his heartbeat synchronizing with the voices, his body beginning to rock slightly in time to the rhythmic beat. He knew that the chant was intended to focus the effect of the drug. It was an old Dervish trick. The colors before his eyes seemed to intensify, the reds and yellows and oranges of the flames becoming more distinct, reflecting from the shining sweaty faces of the knights, giving the scene a truly hellish air.

There was a stirring in the back of the room, and one

of the prisoners was led forward. It was the youth whom de Beaumont had been fondling earlier. His hands were tied behind him and his face was a mask of terror. By a rope halter around his neck, he was dragged forward to the altar. At the altar, he stood behind the stone slab facing the crowd. His hands were untied and his clothes stripped from him. His skin was white and unmarked.

With a hand at the back of the youth's head, Marco shoved him forward to lie bent across the stone. His arms were tied to rings on the forward side and his ankles on the other. The men, now chanting frenziedly, looked to de Beaumont. He raised his hands in benediction. "Begin, my children."

Standing behind the youth, Marco yanked his black robe over his head. The Lombard knight was as grossly erect as the statue behind him. He seized the boy's hips and drove himself forward. The maniacal chanting almost drowned out the youth's screams.

When Marco was done with the victim, another took his place, then another. De Beaumont looked up smiling at Falcon's stony face. "When are you going to take your turn, Draco? You are the guest of honor, you know."

Falcon glared at the mad scene before him. The fifth or sixth knight was sodomizing the victim. All over the room, the worshipers were tearing off their garments, seizing one another and rolling about on the straw-covered floor. The chanting had given way to a general howling, gasping, and growling.

Suddenly, with incredible clarity, Falcon saw himself as a young man on his first day in the galley, bent over the ship's rail, his back in bloody ribbons from his first lashing. There came back to him, with astonishing fidelity, the feeling of rage, humiliation, and terror that paled the pain of the flogging as the loathsome Abu approached with his twisted leer, pulling off his loincloth while the crewmen looked on, laughing and clapping.

Then he was back in the chapel, and de Beaumont was still looking at him. He saw once more what they were doing to the boy, who had stopped screaming and fallen unconscious. No. There were some things he could not do, even to gain his vengeance. He looked down into de Beaumont's face, ready to fight for his life in an instant. "I think not, my lord. It's not to my taste." To his surprise, de Beaumont seemed not in the least bit perturbed.

"As you will, Draco. After all, this isn't the most important part of the communion." The Black Pope returned his attention to the infernal scene. Most of the knights were now writhing slowly upon the floor, their crazed passion spent. A last knight was pounding away at the victim, and as he fell away, de Beaumont heaved his bulk from the throne and took his place behind the youth, pulling up his robes in front. What a wonderful opportunity to kill them all, Falcon was thinking. They'd be too fogged with drugs and lust to respond quickly. Just throw some torches down into the straw and then dash to the door to hold them off and watch them all burn. Of course, he would die himself, but it almost seemed worth it.

With a last plunge, de Beaumont grabbed the youth's hair and pulled his head back. Marco handed him a dagger and he drew it across the white throat, drenching the altar to the cheers of the besotted knights. Baphomet looked grimly down, with evident satisfaction. As de Beaumont stepped back, three men came forward with heavy, cleaverlike knives. They began methodically to carve the corpse into small pieces.

De Beaumont returned to the throne, straightening his robes and breathing heavily. He collapsed upon the seat. "Oh, to have the powers of youth again," he said. "You should have joined us, Draco. This keeps us strong. Women weaken a man." Falcon said nothing.

A knight came to Falcon and de Beaumont. He handed each a skewer upon which was impaled a bite-sized chunk of raw meat. Falcon looked at the altar. Nothing remained of the victim except the head, some glistening bones, and a pile of organs and offal. De Beaumont was watching him again.

"This is the true communion, Draco, and in this you must participate." He popped the morsel into his mouth and chewed with evident relish.

Falcon looked at the thing on the wooden sliver he held. So this was how he bound his men to him—with a rite so hideous none of them could ever want to rejoin normal society. Falcon had seen cannibalism before. It always happened at sieges. He could eat it, or he could die. That was the choice. Without taking his eyes from de Beaumont's, he put the piece of flesh in his mouth and withdrew the skewer. Slowly and deliberately, he began chewing.

NINE

"**THERE** are great times ahead, Draco," de Beaumont was saying. They were in de Beaumont's chamber, and light was shining through the windows, and the hellish scene of the night before seemed like an evil dream. For the first time, the Black Pope was speaking to Falcon as if with full confidence. "The world is opening up, and there is nothing that strong men can't accomplish if they have the will!" Falcon was not sure whether the man was talking to him or to some audience that existed only in his own mind.

"You saw the wars in the East, Draco. Never were there such wars, such wholesale butchery! Soon all wars will be on such a scale, not just petty baron against petty baron, or kinglet against kinglet, but entire nations, whole peoples locked in a struggle to the annihilation of one or the other. Only the strong and ruthless can win in this new world, Draco. Only those who are willing to forswear all weakness can prevail. The Christian way is outdated. When I was a prince of that religion, most of my fellow bishops spent half their time thinking up ways to make the barons' little wars fit in with Christ's teachings." He laughed humorlessly. "For twelve hundred years we've wasted our ingenuity trying to reconcile a teaching of peace and love and passivity to our natural desire to kill and subdue and dominate. I have done with such hypocrisy! Baphomet is the god of human nature. He increases the strength of those who worship him. The only purpose of the weak is to serve the strong!" He gesticulated wildly, and didn't notice when a small key fell from his sash. Draco saw it but gave no indication.

"I'm glad you've joined us, Draco," he ranted on, "because I think you're a man like me. A superior man. A man who is willing to discard the old, limiting ways when they no longer suit his ambitions. With Baphomet, there is no limit to what you can achieve; wealth, land, boys, women if you want them, and most of all"—his fingers writhed into clenched fists—"power. To set your foot upon the necks of your enemies and take their goods and to see their people fall on their faces in terror at your approach. To hear them sing your praises not in admiration, but in fear. Remember that, Draco," he lectured now like a schoolmaster. "The only admiration which has value is that of your peers. From inferiors, you want only fear and obedience. Most men are too stupid and foolish to understand anything except their own safety, so obedience must be enforced with terror.

"All of the old teachings must be eliminated." He began ticking points off on his fingers. "Return good for evil? There is no evil and no good, only your own desires. Turn the other cheek? It's the philosophy of weakness and cowardice. Never let your enemy strike you! Always strike him first and make sure that he has no chance to strike you back." De Beaumont drained his winecup and held it out to be filled again. Falcon obliged.

"I tell you, Draco, we can become the masters of the world. With a clear perception of strength and the uses of power and the weakness and degeneracy of most of humanity, we can bring about a new age, an age of fire and steel and the absolute rule of the man who has neither pity nor compunction. What, after all, is pity, except the invention of natural slaves in order to sap the pure ruthlessness of the strong?"

For the first time, Falcon interrupted the harangue. "We'll need greater numbers in order to master the world, don't you think, my lord?"

"Our numbers will grow," de Beaumont prophesied. "But we have more than mere numbers. We have the strength of our Master, who will deliver our enemies into our hands. You will see, Draco! My Black Army has the strength of pure will. What does it matter if the Christians have greater numbers? With my will and leadership and your military skills, how can they stand against us? They will scatter like chaff before the wind!"

De Beaumont, Falcon thought, was clearly as mad as a flea trying to mount an elephant. Somehow, in spite of all his experience, he had forgotten just how incredibly brutal and ferocious those "weak" Christian armies and barons could be. Falcon himself had never observed that the profession of Christianity had ever abated the savagery of the European warrior nobility in the slightest, no matter how the priests sometimes tried to limit the endless wars. Most barons would cheerfully accept excommunication rather than forgo a single day of warfare. Somehow, de Beaumont had come to actually confuse the words in the Bible with the way Christians really behaved.

"And just what kind of help are we to expect from our Master?" Falcon asked.

De Beaumont's breathing slowed, and he regained his cherubic smile. "Ah, that's the point. We worship our Master, and we give him the blood of his enemies. We sacrifice them to him upon the altars of their own churches. Blood makes him grow strong, Draco, and in return he shares this strength with us. Baphomet is an old god, older than Christ by far. For long, he has subsisted upon the trickles given him by his few adherents. Now, we of the Brethren are feeding him torrents, and his power grows daily. When we set out to descend upon the Christian world, we will hold one grand mass sacrifice, and this will render us invincible."

"Grand sacrifice?" Falcon said. "But how? You bring back no prisoners, no—" He paused as understanding took hold of him.

"That's right, Draco," said de Beaumont. "I see you know already. I always said that you had a quick mind. Yes, that's why we've spared the villagers so far. Soon we'll begin to round them up. We'll pen them up like cattle and on the proper day we'll begin the slaughter."

"How many?" Falcon asked, appalled.

De Beaumont shrugged. "Who can say? We'll scour these valleys and flush them from wherever they're hiding. There must be at least ten thousand in the villages on these slopes. We'll cast a wide net."

"Ten thousand," Falcon said. "Even Richard's two thousand slaughtered prisoners at Acre will seem small by comparison."

"Yes," said de Beaumont, chuckling, "it will be most pleasing to our Master. Too bad about Richard. He has real promise, but he's too besotted with Christianity and chivalry to be of any use to us. If only we could have taken him in while he was still young enough to teach, he could have been the greatest of us all."

Falcon let himself into the room quietly. De Beaumont was occupied with secret matters in the chapel. He might never have another chance to search the room. The light was fading, but he had had no trouble finding the key among the straw on the floor. But was it the right one? He crossed to the chest and tried it. The lock opened easily. He threw back the lid and began taking out books carefully, noting where each had lain so that he could replace it exactly as found. Many were books of occult scholarship, some of which he recognized from having seen their like in Suleiman's and Abraham's libraries. One bore upon its spine the title *The Secret Book of the Templars*. He longed to look into that one, but he had more immediate matters in mind. Then he found a stack of letters. Some were in Arabic, others in Latin, still others in various vernacular tongues. Most of these latter Falcon found almost impossible to decipher quickly, even where he knew the language. Spelling and grammar were pretty much at the pleasure of the writer and the simplest message could take hours to figure out.

Then a seal caught his eye. It was one he had not seen in many years, bearing a stylized depiction of a hill cleft by a sword. It was the seal of Nigel Edgehill, one of his father's betrayers. He tore it open and read avidly. Fortunately, it was written in Latin, though the language was not classical, but mediocre church Latin written by an indifferent scribe. Translating as he read, he scanned an involved greeting and introduction until he came to the meat of the message: "Gunther Valdemar is dead. Our brother perished at the hands of a mercenary knight at the siege of an obscure castle in the South of France. Valdemar was always the least among us, a Teutonic pig if ever there was one. The peculiar thing about his demise is the man who killed him. The sell-sword calls himself Draco Falcon. The name is similar to Draco de Montfalcon, whom we believed dead long ago. If it is he, then it will be as if old Eudes were back. I don't know how Draco could have survived the galleys, but then none of us in England expected to see Richard again, either, after the Austrian took him. Keep on your guard. If it is Draco, he will be tracking us down. Our Master keep and protect you." There was no signature except for the seal. Edgehill was as illiterate as most nobles.

That was all the message. No indication of where it had been sent from, or where Edgehill might be now. No mention of Odo FitzRoy. At least he knew that Edgehill was still alive. He'd have been disappointed to find the man dead before he could catch up with him. Now, though, he had another problem. De Beaumont must have known all along that he had killed Valdemar, but had tried to enlist him anyway. He had put Falcon through the grotesque ceremony, had tested him—the key! *That* had been the real test. It had not fallen from de Beaumont's robe accidentally. He had to get away from here, and soon. He heard footsteps on the gallery outside.

"Can't read, eh?" It was de Beaumont's voice, muffled by the thick wood of the door. "Really, Draco, my boy, I'm disappointed in you. I'd had great hopes for you. If only you'd been open with me from the beginning, and told me about your little encounter with Valdemar, I'd have trusted your word. Did you really think I'd have held that German pig's life against the son of my old friend Eudes? I'm afraid my trust is at an end, though. Disarm yourself and come out quietly if you'd live."

Slowly, silently, Falcon drew Nemesis and took her long grip in both hands. "I'm coming out, my lord," he said. "I can explain everything."

"I hope so, Draco. Now just—" Abruptly, the door slammed open and a black-mailed warrior leaped into the room. A swift slash of the curved blade took his sword hand off at the wrist and a shove from Falcon's foot sent the screaming man reeling back out among his fellows, toppling two of them. With a howling warcry, Falcon was out on the gallery among them. The gallery was crowded with men, all armed and armored, but for this kind of fighting none wore the barrel helms or carried shields.

Falcon was caught in the grip of a ferocious joy. He had degraded himself and his father's memory by living among them. Now he was going to make them pay. As the two fallen men tried to rise, a single swipe of Nemesis slit both their throats, and suddenly the footing on the gallery became treacherous. Two men darted in from the sides, and Falcon took one out with a terrific overhand blow that shredded mail and flesh. He felt a sting from behind as the other's sword skittered across his mailed back, and he whirled, smashing the crescent pommel into the man's face, relishing the crunch of bone beneath the heavy bronze. Men were falling back in both directions now, unwilling to face this superhuman fury.

"Take him, you cowards!" Marco shouted. "He's only one man!" Marco and de Beaumont stood behind a crowd of knights, both furiously urging them on.

Falcon jumped to the railing and stood atop it, and as the knights closed in he dropped down into the courtyard, landing with his knees bent to take up the shock. Two more warriors rushed him to take advantage of his momentary imbalance. Both were disemboweled for their impetuosity. The men in the courtyard had not been expecting anything like this, and Falcon rushed to the gate, cutting down any rash enough to try to stop him. The attacks of the heavy-mailed knights seemed pathetically slow in comparison to Falcon's lightning fury.

"Power, de Beaumont?" Falcon shouted. "Strength? I'll show you what strength means!" The old madness was taking hold of him, the thing that Suleiman had tried to control. He reached the gate so swiftly that the courtyard might as well have been unoccupied. Falcon scrambled up the steps leading to the wallwalk, a pack of baying knights at his heels. He turned at the top of the steps and sent the leaders tumbling back with a furious kick, then turned to the wall. To his surprise, a grappling hook chunked into the stones atop the wall. He looked over and saw a man gesticulating toward him, holding the rope attacked to the hook. He slammed Nemesis home in her sheath and scrambled over the wall, sliding down the rope to the ground below.

"We've been waiting for you these ten days and more, my lord." It was Donal MacFergus, and never was Falcon happier to see one of his men. The two sprinted for the high ground, where they could not be followed by men on horseback. As they ran, the Irishman chided him for his recklessness. "Been out here day and night, in all weathers, Draco. Why'd you take so long? Playing about in that madman's abbey while honest soldiers have been watching out for you. It's a disgrace." The chiding words were the Irishman's way of expressing his joy at having his lord back, and Falcon let him run on for a while until they were safely hidden among the rocks.

"Peace, Donal," he said, at length. "How many are you? Are the rest of the men here yet?"

"Nah, just the two of us, Wulf and me. And a few of the villagers—good lads, but they'll take some training. The Old Woman's been busy, but these folk are slow to rise."

"Lilitha?" Falcon said. "Did she escape, that night in Goatsfoot?"

"That she did. She's a rare one, she is. Hard as any man I ever knew, and a good deal wiser than you, begging your pardon. If the rest were like her, these madmen in black iron would soon be no trouble to anybody. If my lord were a wise man, which all the world knows he's not, he'd marry that wench and we'd have between them something to amount to one fine leader."

"Don't go making matches for your betters," said Falcon, appending a good-natured but solid kick to the Irishman's backside. "Just lead me to Wulf and the lady and these mountain warriors of yours. Time's short if we're to do something about de Beaumont."

The Irishman turned serious once more. "Have we any

chance? We sent Simon and the Welshmen to fetch the lads, but they've not returned yet."

"Just show me what you've got," Falcon said, "and I'll tell you what our chances are."

"Everyone?" Lilitha said. "He really plans to sacrifice everyone in these mountains to this god of his?" The idea was too much for her to take in. "But why? They have no fields to till. They raise no flocks or herds, they only take what others have raised. The purpose of blood sacrifice is to ensure the fertility of the coming year. Blood pays for blood. What can this goat-man-god give them, and why does he thirst so for blood?" The two sat in an isolated goatherd's hut far from the fortress. All around were scattered the little force Lilitha had raised. A low fire burned in a hearth of river stones, its light well masked from view.

"As I've said, they're mad," Falcon explained. "What de Beaumont wants is power. He thirsts for power more than any man I've ever seen."

"Power?" she said, puzzled. "Do you mean magical power? The ability to perform great spells?"

"No, it's something else he wants. It's power over other men. He wants to see them bow down to him. He wants the power of life and death, and to have the destinies of nations at his whim."

"But what does he gain from that?" She knelt next to the hearth. The season was advancing, and the night was warm. The fire was small, just enough to provide light.

"It's a sickness, Lilitha, one I've seen before, but never to so great a degree." Stripped to his hose and shirt, Falcon half reclined against the bag that held his rolled-up mailshirt. In his hand was a flagon of ale. "Most men of power are born to it. As often as not, they find it a burden they'd as soon be rid of. But the world outside these mountains is a savage place, with each man's hand raised

125

against every other. Only by seizing a share of power can a man hold some degree of security for himself and his family. The only alternative is to put himself under the protection of a stronger man, but then he loses freedom to act.

"Most men find some middle ground—my own men are like that. They serve me, and obey my commands. By doing this they escape being bound to the soil like serfs. They have a guarantee of a livelihood and a more interesting life than most. I am my own master, except when I'm serving someone for pay. That way, I have much time free to accomplish what I must. Freest of all are the kings, the emperor, the Pope, the sultans and such. At least, they seem free. Anyone who has lived among them, though, knows that they are as bound by conventions and limitations as anyone else. They must endure endless ceremonies, raise taxes, soothe fractious barons, marry for political advantage, engage in diplomacy with their neighbors; the list is endless."

"Then why does de Beaumont want such a life?"

"Because he's a self-deluded fool. I think I'm beginning to understand him, though. He wasn't born to power. He's the younger son of some minor Flemish noble, pledged early to the church. Through hard work and ambition, he earned the rank of archbishop. Very few men without powerful family connections could have done that. He knew that he was as high as he would ever get. It takes real wealth to buy into the College of Cardinals, and a man has to be wealthy and powerfully connected and an Italian to become Pope. De Beaumont couldn't stand such limitations on his vaunting ambition.

"Men like de Beaumont are eaten up every day of their lives with envy. He sees himself as a great man, whose rightful power and station are withheld from him by men whose only qualification is superior birth. In his delusion, he sees none of the responsibilities of power; only its exercise and abuse. He wants the rewards of power, but none of its burdens.

"He thinks himself capable of the powers not of a king but of a god. Somehow, in Palestine, he came across this ancient obscenity and believed that it was the answer to his lust for power. To men like him, the deaths of thousands, or of tens or hundreds of thousands, are as nothing. Other men serve only to satisfy his wants. Men have tried to rule like that before. I learned of them when I served Suleiman the Wise. Nero was one such, and a man called Caligula. Men remember them as the mad rulers, and none of them lasted very long. That never deters others from dreaming their dreams, though."

Lilitha studied him. These names meant nothing to her, and much of what Falcon was saying passed beyond her. He was using too many words unfamiliar to her, and he spoke of matters of which she had no understanding; wars and ambitions and the struggle for power. As far as she could tell, what he was describing was the need of some men to do evil and be hated. At least it was comforting to believe that Falcon had some understanding of the terrifying events that had descended upon her mountains and people.

She was seeing a new side of Falcon. Before, there had been only the warrior, the killer of men who was driven by an obsession almost as mad as that of the rebel archbishop. This was a different man; a man who could read, and who had listened to the teachings of wise men. This was a man who thought deeply and who could put himself in the place of his deadly enemy in order to understand the man. It was the very antithesis of the savage, instinctive fighter who was also Draco Falcon.

In her untutored but intuitive fashion, she could make a far shrewder analysis of Falcon than could he himself. She saw two sides of him now, and she suspected that there were many more. She knew him to be strong, fierce, ambitious, and obsessed, as well as intelligent and a little mad. With a chill, she realized that in some ways he resembled de Beaumont.

Falcon sat sipping his ale and staring moodily into the fire. Another of his mercurial changes of mood had come over him. He was through talking. "Tomorrow," he said, "we see to drilling the men and getting the defenses together."

"I'll make the rounds of the villages again," said Lilitha. "Now that I know what the black riders plan to do, I think the people will rise up."

"They'd better," Falcon said grimly. Then yet another light came into his eyes, as he remembered something that he had left unfinished. He reached out and stroked her raven hair, running his hand down to cup her cheek. Lilitha closed her eyes, then turned her head into his hand and licked his palm. His hand slid down her neck to her shoulder and freed the bone peg, as she released the other. The dress caught on her breasts, and she shook her shoulders to make it fall. The white mounds continued to quiver for several moments after the wool fell to her waist. Falcon untied the knot of her belt and pulled her upright as he pushed the fabric down, sliding his hands down over the rich curves of her hips and along her thighs to the knees.

Lilitha pulled at the laces of his shirt and drew it up over his head. "Stand up," she said, her voice trembling. They both stood, and she loosened the cord that held his hose. She knelt to strip them from his legs. The smoky air in the hut was warm on his skin, but he wouldn't have noticed a blizzard. This time, there were no thoughts of other women. He started to pull her over to the heap of stuffed skins in the corner, but she put a hand on his chest.

"Wait," she said. She stood on tiptoe to pull his head down. He thought she wanted him to kiss her breast, but instead she took his face between her hands and said, "There is power here." Beginning at his hairline, her tongue traced the lightning scar, down across his face to his chin, then down his neck and across his chest, following the thin line where it whitened the hair. She dropped to her knees to trace the line down his belly to his groin. Her tongue burned almost as the lightning had, and Falcon's breath came so hard that he feared the men outside would hear. There was power here indeed, but it was not of the kind that de Beaumont dreamed.

Lilitha's tongue continued to follow the line down his inner thigh to the side of the calf, finally dropping to all fours to trace it to its end at his heel. She raised herself to her knees and embraced his thighs. She laid her cheek against his belly, and her breath was hot on his manhood as she took its length in her hand and stroked it. Then she pulled back and with a shudder he felt her mouth close warmly over him. He held her head between his hands, stroking her silken hair between his fingers.

When he could bear her ministrations no longer, he bent and picked her up, holding her as lightly as if she had been a child, with one hand behind her neck and the other beneath her buttocks. Her arms went around his neck and they kissed long and deeply. Her arms fell to hang limply behind her and her head dropped back as he raised her in his arms and took first one nipple and then the other in his mouth, stroking them with his tongue until they extended into hard points, excruciatingly sensitive. Then he teased her navel with his tongue and her belly writhed in time to her hard breathing, and at last she gasped, "Now!"

He took her to the pallet and laid her gently upon it. He was about to lie between her legs when she doubled her thighs back until they pressed against her breasts. She slid her feet past his shoulders and crossed her ankles behind his neck. He braced himself on outstretched hands as she reached down between them. With one hand she parted her dense-furred flesh and with the other guided him into her. With a lunge that drove the breath from both of them, he buried himself in her. Then the ancient, ritual dance began.

They were both lovers of long experience, and both had been deprived for too long. After the first coupling, fierce and passionate and over much too quick, they made love again and then a third time, their bodies rearranging themselves over and over, as they sought to wring every last possibility of pleasure and satisfaction from each other's body. Falcon was amazed to find that none of the refinements he had learned in the East were unknown to this woman from an obscure mountain village. She was adept as he and had absolutely no inhibitions in the giving and taking of pleasure between man and woman. Her natural, elemental love cleansed him of the perverted horror he had participated in at the black rider's chapel.

At the end, Falcon was kneeling with Lilitha's legs wrapped around his waist and her body lying back along his thighs, her arms spread out on the pallet and her head whipping from side to side as she gasped, moaned, laughed and wept all at once. With a last, shuddering groan, Falcon pulled her hips to him, his big hands gripping her waist and pulling her against him so tight that she felt her loins being crushed as his face twisted in sweet agony and his seed pumped into her. Then he collapsed to lie on his side, one arm under her, holding her to him as her legs still held them together, his flesh still one with hers.

When her heart had ceased its frantic thudding and his breathing had returned to normal, she stroked his hair. "Stay inside me," she whispered. "What you've put in me I don't want to lose too soon, before it has a chance to work its magic." She smiled and gently licked his ear, this time as a loving caress and not as an incitement to greater passion. "I pray that you have put a child in me, a strong child that will live."

"By God, my love," Falcon said, his voice hoarse with the power of his expended passion, "I think I must have put three in you, at least." He hugged her to him even more closely. Slowly, so as not to disturb their joining, she drew her lower leg out from under him. The other stayed across his hip. Exhausted, joined together in the most ancient of bonds, they slept.

TEN

"**B**EGGIN' your lordships shit-soaked pardon, but will you tell them nun-fuckers to be out of my fucking way or shall I use my little hammer here to knock the dogshit out from between their ears?" Rupert Foul-Mouth waved his massive wooden maul in the face of the officious horseman who stood in his path. Also in his path were twenty men armed with glaives—long, curved cutting blades mounted on poles.

The opposing horseman drew himself up in his saddle. He wore a sword but no armor. "My lord's orders are most strict: While the hosting is being held for the Crusade against the black demons, no armed force may cross the border." He looked critically at the small but heavily armed force that was quickly approaching behind Rupert. "Especially a pack of ruffians who would bear watching and require an armed escort at the best of times."

"I'll escort your shriveled balls all the way to—" Rupert was cut off by the arrival of a splendidly armored man mounted on a destrier. At his waist was an exceptionally long sword. The sword was named Moorslayer and its wearer was Sir Ruy Ortiz, Falcon's master of horse. Propped on his saddle was the staff of a long banner, depicting a spread-winged falcon gripping bolts of blue lightning in its talons.

"Hold, Rupert," Ortiz said. He then addressed the official. "Sir, I beg your pardon if this man has spoken discourteously to you. It is just his manner."

"Courteous or discourteous, my orders from my lord are to let no armed force pass until the matter of the mountain demons has been settled."

"Most loyal!" said Sir Ruy. "If only every man did his duty by his liege so well! It strikes me, sir, that there is an honorable solution to this problem. We will find armor for you, and you and I can go to that field yonder and joust. If I am victorious, we shall pass and no honor has been lost. I'll see to it that your name is mentioned in the poem I shall compose when I retire from the wars. Are you of noble rank or knightly station?"

"I am not," the man answered, now slightly pale.

"Oh," said Sir Ruy, disappointed. He turned to the old siege engineer. "Go ahead and kill him, Rupert. I'll drive off this rabble." Just then two more horsemen arrived. One was Simon, the other was Rudolph of Austria. Rudolph was in the act of drawing his sword, named Cheeseparer.

"Wait!" Simon shouted. "Rudolph, put up your sword." He turned to the official. "Sir, I spoke to your lord some weeks ago. We are the men of Sir Draco Falcon. Even now, our lord is up in the mountains, at the mercy of those monsters, and we ride to his rescue. Didn't your lord tell you to watch for this banner?" He pointed at the standard borne by Sir Ruy.

"Hmm," the official grumbled. He took a folded parchment from his belt and opened it, studying several small shields painted upon it in colors. "Mm, well, yes, here it is: a black falcon, holding blue thunderbolts in his talons."

"You ill-bred lout!" screamed Sir Ruy. "In *her* talons! The falcon is the female bird! The male is a tiercel!" He began drawing his sword at this insult to his beloved banner.

The official flushed crimson in mortification. A commoner, he knew nothing of falconry.

"Oh, put up, Ruy," Simon said disgustedly. "We're wasting precious time here." He turned to the official. "May we pass?" The man signaled to his men, and they drew aside with expressions of profound relief.

He watched as the small force crossed the border. It was unlike any force he had ever seen. Instead of the usual feudal array of cavalry and footmen, these were all mounted, though many were clearly soldiers who fought on foot. Weapons and armor were all clean and polished, and he saw no speck of rust. Instead of straggling along with each man riding at whatever pace suited him, the men rode in neat double file, each pair of horsemen an even ten paces from the pair before and behind. They reminded him of tales he had heard from returning Crusaders of the Greek emperor's armies, which always rode and marched in this disciplined fashion.

Behind the horsemen came a siege train, its equipment dismantled and stowed neatly on wagons. For a wonder, the wagons were pulled by horses instead of oxen. These were obviously warhorses past their prime but still strong enough to pull loads. He had never seen horses hitched to wagons before. He had expected to see a rabble of camp-followers draggling along behind the armed men, but this army had none. Within minutes, they were out of sight. Ordinarily, even an array as small as this took half a day to pass a given point. They were something new in his world, but he had a feeling that he hadn't seen the last of their kind.

Falcon supervised the workers as they stacked stones across the narrow valley from one side to the other. Five hundred yards uphill, Donal was seeing to the building of a second. The same distance past that, Wulf was finishing work on a third. Work parties of boys and girls were bringing back sacks full of fist-sized stones and piling them at intervals behind the walls.

On the long, open slope before the first wall, Lilitha and the village women were planting short wooden stakes, driving them deep into the earth at an angle pointing forward, against the enemy. When each was firmly seated, its end was whittled to a sharp point. Already the field was densely studded with them, enough to slow the charge of the most determined cavalry.

For three days, the men and women and older children of Goatsfoot and a few other villages had been carrying on this unaccustomed labor. The people of the other villages had been warned to take their children and their livestock and flee to the security of the high mountain valleys. They would have to endure the cold of the crags still locked in snow, but they would be safe from the depredations of the riders. Already, some of the young men of those villages were coming down to join the fighters, having seen to the safety of their loved ones.

Wulf came bounding down the slope to stand at Falcon's side, panting in the thin mountain air. "Third wall's done, my lord," he said. Falcon was gazing up at the mist that gathered overhead every day at this time. For about fifty paces uphill, the flanking slopes were plain to see, the air perfectly clear. Then they disappeared above the seemingly solid ceiling of fog. "What are you looking at?" Wulf asked.

"The mist," Falcon said. "It's at just that height, every day, regular as sunrise, and it stays there till morning."

"So it is," said Wulf, looking at the fog and scratching his head. "What of it?"

"Wulf, Wulf," Falcon said, shaking his head. "Haven't I told you always to be aware of the terrain and its possibilities? Haven't I told you that water and rain and snow are as important as rocks and trees and slopes?"

"You have," Wulf agreed. "But what good is fog to anybody?"

"To us, it's a gift from heaven. We're going to make use of that fog when de Beaumont comes."

Lilitha came to join them. "The stakes are all planted, Draco." Despite the labor she was performing, she wore her finest gown, dyed with rare mountain herbs, and she wore her necklace, her bracelets, and her arm rings. She was the Old Woman, and her people had to be kept aware of that.

"Good," Falcon said. "We're almost ready, as soon as this wall's finished." He surveyed his hasty fortifications. "When they charge, we'll take out as many as we can. When we can hold this wall no longer, we'll retreat to the next, then to the third. As our numbers get fewer, the walls will get shorter, so we can keep the same density of defense and prevent gaps in our line."

"Will we lose many?" Lilitha asked.

"Some," Falcon said, "but not ten thousand."

Wulf pointed to a man who was running up the slope below them. It was the hunter who had guided them on their first visit to the fortress. He rushed to Lilitha's side and gasped out a report in the mountain tongue.

"The riders have ridden into some of the deserted villages," Lilitha translated. "They found nothing. Most are riding back to the abbey; the rest are still searching in small bands. The watch on the gorge reports no sight of your men."

"They'll find us soon," Falcon said. "But it's too late in the day to attack now. That's good. We'll all get a good night's rest."

Donal joined the little group. "Second wall's done, my

lord. I've seen desperate measures, but this is a prizewinner: throwing rocks at armored knights from behind farmyard dikes." The Irishman caught sight of something downslope and shaded his eyes against the glare of the setting sun to see. "There's two of the loonies," he reported. They all strained their eyes to make out the figures made tiny by distance. There was no question. Two black-armored horsemen were standing in their stirrups, staring up at them.

"They know where we are now," Wulf said. "Shall we go down there and try to kill them?"

"They're already riding away," Falcon said. "Get the fires started. Have everybody eat and then get some sleep. We'll be up early tomorrow, and it'll be a long day. A short one, for some."

"What do you think, my lord—can we really defeat them this way?" Donal was clearly skeptical.

"No," Falcon said, with a firm shake of his head. "We can hurt them; slow them down. The only way to defeat them is to bottle them up in their castle and scour them out. This buys us time."

"Time," Donal said glumly. Never since the eternal hell of the galley had time seemed so much his enemy.

Accompanied only by Lilitha, Falcon made an inspection of the stakes she and the other women had planted. He wanted to make use of every minute of the fading daylight. He placed his mailed arm around Lilitha's shoulders, and she reached up to cover his hand with hers, savoring its human warmth. She could never accustom herself to the embrace of the cold iron. They had had only the one night together, and then they had been too busy for more than an occasional touch or a quick kiss as they passed one another, rushing to their desperate tasks. She placed a hand on her belly, hoping that his seed had found fertile ground.

"What happens after tomorrow?" she asked.

"The battle is not over tomorrow, even if we both live."

"But when the fighting is past, what will you do then?" She gripped his hand tightly as they walked back toward the glimmering light of the campfires.

"Lilitha," he said, "it's bad luck to think beyond the next battle." He took her in his arms and wrapped his heavy cloak around them both. Not wanting him to know, she wept against his chest, hating the iron that covered it, loving the heart the iron protected. Even through the mail and leather, she could hear its powerful beating.

The morning dawned clear and bright. The people behind the low stone walls scanned the slopes and nervously hefted the fist-sized rocks or tested their slings for the hundredth time. They had already eaten, and Falcon had ordered the fires put out. He didn't want people backing into hot embers as they retreated from wall to wall. The retreating was the part that bothered him. All the songs were written about charges and successful advances. Nobody sang about retreats, but Falcon knew that an orderly retreat was one of the most difficult of military maneuvers. All too easily, it could turn into a rout, with the men dropping their weapons and running in panic, presenting their backs to the enemy and being cut down at the enemy's pleasure.

He had instructed and drilled them, but they weren't professional soldiers, and only professionals could be counted on to follow orders. He surveyed his little "army." They looked tough, he had to grant them that. They were keyed up for battle, but they seemed unafraid. In their rough woolen garments, with their shaggy, unshorn hair, they had an air of primitive tenacity. They were not warlike, but they would fight to defend their lives. He hoped that de Beaumont would find these people an entirely different proposition from those villagers below, who were so used to the oppression of the armored aristocracy that they permitted themselves to be slaughtered like sheep.

Lilitha, Wulf, and Donal stood by Falcon as he leaned on the first wall and watched the slope, waiting for the appearance of the black horsemen. A woman arrived and handed Lilitha a long leather bag. She handed it to Falcon. "Here is the horn you wanted."

Falcon stripped the bag from the horn. It was an ancient instrument, made of hammered bronze and decorated with figures embossed in repoussée. The figures were animal and human, but he didn't recognize the style. The horn was about a yard long, most of its length straight until it turned sharply upward at the bell. Horns like this were used for signaling across the mountain crevasses, and were supposed to produce a tone that would not set off an avalanche. He set his lips to the mouthpiece and tried a blast. The sound was low-pitched and eerie.

"Not very loud," Falcon said. "Do you think it will be heard above the sounds of the battle?"

"The sound of these horns carries far," Lilitha said. "You can sound one from one side of a waterfall and it can be heard clearly on the other side."

"It will have to do. Wulf, do you and your men know what to do?"

"How not?" Wulf said, nettled. "You drilled us hard enough." He nervously swished his falchion in practice cuts. The short curved sword had the mottled sheen that identified a Damascus blade. In his left hand he held a small round shield by its central handle. It was designed to parry blows or sweep them aside rather than block them as a big horseman's shield did.

Donal cradled his ax in his big, scarred fists. The ax was of traditional Irish design, narrow at the eye through which the handle passed, flaring out to a wide, curved cutting edge. It was lighter than most battle axes, and a strong man could swing it easily with one hand. Its handle was as long as Donal's arm and gracefully and subtly curved. They had cut down the two lances they had taken from the riders at the gorge, shortening them by about a third of their length, a handy size for footmen. One of these lances was propped in front of Donal. Wulf had the other.

Falcon regretted not having his ax. Nemesis was a precision weapon, not ideal for the kind of melee they were facing. As a substitute he had had a club made: a heavy rock lashed to a four-foot pole. He circled it about his head a few times in practice, twirling the ponderous weapon as easily as if it were a willow wand.

"Here they come," Donal said quietly. Below them, a file of the black riders rode into the broad meadow. Then the grass was covered with them.

"Lilitha," Falcon said, "go back up beyond the third wall and stay there with the women."

"I want to be here with you," she said.

"This is man's work, and it'll be an ugly, bloody business. You'd be no use here and I'll have no thought to spare for you once the fighting starts. Do as I say." Then, in a softer voice: "You are the Old Woman, Lilitha. If we are destroyed here today, you must lead what's left of your people to safety."

"You are right," she said.

When Lilitha was gone, the men watched grimly as the array of riders advanced, in no particular order. At their head rode a huge figure who bore a spiked club. Alone of all the riders, his helm was perfectly plain and without ornament.

"De Beaumont," Falcon whispered, flexing his fingers on the shaft of his makeshift weapon. "You're mine, now."

As expected, the horsemen sent no scouts ahead. It was unknightly to worry about what was ahead or search out the terrain. Likewise, they would expect no resistance from mere peasants, whom they would expect to break and run the first second they saw the knights charging. That was all to the good.

Falcon stood atop the wall and waved at them. From the black riders came an unearthly collective howl.

"Souls in hell must sound like that," Donal muttered.

De Beaumont stared through his narrow eye slits at the ragged band behind the wall. There was Draco, waving a big club over his head. De Beaumont pulled his helmet off to get a good breath of air before the fighting began. Not that this pitiful force was likely to call for much fighting. Marco rode up and reined in beside his master. Marco's helm was crested with a spread-winged dragon, its claws clutching the sides of the helm and its spined tail dropping down the back to his shoulder blades. De Beaumont signaled for the Lombard to unhelm so that they could talk.

"I want that man taken alive, if at all possible," de Beaumont said, pointing to Falcon. "We'll have him bent over the altar at our next ceremony, Marco."

"Yes, my lord," Marco said eagerly. His flushed face and rapid breath betrayed the effect of the drug they had all taken prior to riding out.

"Making him our communion will strengthen us all," de Beaumont said. "If he will not be one of us, then he can become part of us all. I think he is the strongest and most cunning warrior of our time, Marco. You and the others may have the rest, but I will eat his heart." He turned his attention to more immediate matters.

"We'll advance slowly. There's no sense charging against a wall, even if it's a low one. They can't do us much harm in any case, Draco's had too little time to train them as he did those others you encountered." He pointed up the slope, where the points of the stakes were just visible above the grass. "Look there. He's set up some sort of hedgehog, so go through it carefully." Marco nodded furiously, only half hearing. He was eager to come to grips with his enemy, to catch and kill. He rammed his helm down over his mail coif and waited for the signal.

De Beaumont redonned his own helm and rode ahead. He wheeled his horse and faced the men. Raising high his spiked club, he brought it down in a sweep that ended with it pointing back toward the wall. "In the name of the Black Pope and our master, Baphomet: Advance!" He wheeled his mount and set out upslope at a steady canter. It was unlikely that any of the men had heard him, but the example was enough.

Soon, a line of knights was abreast of him. Then a number of them drew ahead. Some broke into a trot, then all of them were trotting. "Slow down, you fools!" de Beaumont shouted, but his loudest bellow went unheard. In their drugged state, it was unlikely that his orders would have had much effect even if they had been heard. "There is no need for a charge!"

"Just as you said," Wulf observed. The villagers seemed subdued, but Wulf, Falcon and Donal watched the approaching line with grim smiles.

"There's no keeping knights from charging," Falcon said, "even if it's uphill onto unknown ground against a wall. It's a good thing they're not Saracens, though." Saracens, mounted on fleet mares or geldings, would simply have leaped over the wall. The knightly greathorse was another matter. Bred for strength and stamina, the horses and their armored riders were too heavy to jump, so they were never trained for it.

"Just a little farther, my beauties," Donal urged in a crooning voice. Then the first horses were going down, their hooves or legs injured by the wooden stakes. The air was torn by the heartrending screams of the steeds.

"Why can't we ever do this without killing the horses?" asked Wulf of nobody in particular. Even then he was cheered by the sight of a black horseman being pitched from his saddle to fall among the stakes. The fallen men were in more danger from the horses' hooves than from the stakes, because their heavy mail prevented most of the points from penetrating. The charge was beginning to stagger and lose its momentum.

As soon as they were within range, the slingers began casting their stones among the riders. Against the shields and helmets of the knights the slingstones were futile. The mail and the thick padding worn under it preserved the knights' limbs and bodies from anything worse than bruises when the stones struck. The horses were another matter. Struck on the head, a horse usually fell. When they were hit on the body, the effect could be even more demoralizing. Knights would ride only stallions, and the stallion's fighting instincts were no less fierce than those of its rider. An injured horse would turn on the nearest mount, biting and kicking.

By the time they reached the wall, the horses had slowed to a walk. Without the momentum of the charge, the lances were nearly useless, so the riders cast them like javelins. They scored few hits, for the long lances were not balanced for throwing. Now the knights began to draw their swords and swing their axes and maces, trying to come to grips with the elusive foe on the other side of the wall.

As Falcon had instructed them, the villagers stepped well back from the wall, continuing to ply their slings. Others were picking up the fallen lances and running back to the second wall with them. Falcon kept back from the wall until he saw two riders occupied with harassing foes on opposite sides of their horses. In an instant, Falcon sprang atop the wall between the two and swung his club in two short, vicious arcs, sending both men to the ground with smashed bones. Before any other could engage him, he was back out of range again.

Wulf and Donal, the only others in any way equipped to deal with the armored men at close quarters, were doing the same. They never tried to engage a man who was in complete control of his mount, or one who could keep his full attention on them.

Soon de Beaumont was riding among his men, cracking his club into the sides of helms to get their attention. "Dismount, you fools!" he shouted. "Dismount and take that wall!"

Eventually, they began to get the idea. One man after another lowered himself from the saddle and strode to the wall.

As the knights began scrambling over the wall, Falcon blew a long blast on the horn. The villagers turned and sprinted for the second wall. It was useless for the heavy-laden knights to try to pursue. They began tearing down the wall to let the horses through.

Behind the protection of the second wall, Falcon and the others took a break to rest and get their wind back. Leaning against the wall were the captured lances. There seemed to be at least seventy of them. These men weren't trained spearmen, but from behind the protection of the wall they should be able to inflict some damage. Falcon got up and hefted one. He thought about the Scots he had heard of, who fought shoulder to shoulder with long spears. The spear was about the simplest and cheapest weapon in the world, and if the spearmen could hold their formation no cavalry could prevail against them. With really long spears, the men wouldn't need much armor, just helmets and maybe light cuirasses or mail shirts for the front line. That way, he mused, even poor men from impoverished countries like Scotland or these mountain valleys could form impressive armies. His ponderings were interrupted by some activity among the knights below. They were remounting.

"To arms!" Falcon called. Without undue hurry, the men were standing to their posts. Their losses had not been as great as Falcon had anticipated and had been confined mostly to those who had been rash enough to try to fight at close quarters with the nearly invulnerable knights. The survivors had gained confidence and were handling themselves uncommonly well. Wulf stood beside Falcon.

"This may not turn out as bad as we'd thought," Wulf said.

"It's not over yet." Falcon looked up. The mist was gathering as it did every day at this time. "Now, do you—"

"Yes," Wulf said resignedly, "as soon as you blow your horn, I'll gather my men and—"

"They're coming!" Donal called. Falcon watched the knights closely. This time they were advancing at a walk, merely using the horses as transportation to convey them to the second wall.

"Damn de Beaumont," Falcon growled. "He has them under control for a change."

"Even the most foolish can learn wisdom if the lessons are hard enough," Wulf observed.

When the knights were within sling range, they dismounted and handed their reins over to men detailed to hold the mounts. Standing in a compact mass, shields held high, the knights advanced under cover toward the wall. The mountaineers saw that their stones were having little effect and picked up the lances.

What followed was a strange battle, in which the spearmen strove to push the armored men away from the wall, while the knights tried to come to close quarters where their hand weapons could have an effect. The result was a struggle that was almost without casualties on either side. Eventually, the sheer weight of the solid block of knights pushed the defenders back. Only Falcon, Wulf, and Donal, all experienced spear fighters, were able to bring down a few of the enemy by placing shrewd thrusts into weak spots on the opposing armor.

Within minutes, knights were forcing themselves over weakly held spaces on the wall. Falcon winded his horn once more. Wulf ran along the defensive line, slapping shoulders. His men followed him toward the third wall. When they were safely away, Falcon blew a second blast. This time, the rest of the mountaineers fell back. Falcon was amazed that these amateurs could behave in such a disciplined fashion. As he retreated, he reflected upon the manner in which they lived. The hard life of the barren mountains bred a people who knew that the slightest oversight, be it in combat or sheepherding, could result in death for the individual or his whole family.

At the third wall, Falcon was gratified to see that not a single lance had been abandoned. Now the village women came down, bringing pots of ale and sacks of bread and cheese for the fighters. As soon as the defenders were refreshed, the women retreated above the mist to rejoin their Old Woman. Falcon took a deep pull at an ale pot, then ate some bread and cheese. No banquet in a lord's castle had ever tasted better. He saw Donal inspecting the defenses.

"Are Wulf and his men—"

"Yes, yes, my lord," the Irishman said. "Stop your fretting. You're worse than an Ulster grandmother for worry. Wulf's a soldier too, you know."

"Don't try to tell me my trade!" Falcon snapped. He knew that Donal was correct. For all their years together, he still thought of Wulf as his horseboy.

The third wall was less than half the length of the first. With the lances so massed, they were able to keep the

146

knights at a distance and not give them a chance to probe for weak spots. Falcon ran back up the slope to scan out over the heads of both defenders and attackers. He saw Marco and de Beaumont at the rear of their men, haranguing and pushing them, trying to employ them to best effect. Falcon bit off a curse. He had been counting upon using the black riders' irrationality against them. That wasn't going to work. They were fighting in a soldierly fashion now. Not as professionally as Falcon or his men might have done, but far better than the usual feudal host. He rejoined the men at the wall, snatching up a lance and thrusting it beneath a helm. This was one of his favorite targets. The point was unlikely to pierce the mail, but it would crush the larynx beneath. He'd lost his club somewhere, and the circumstances still weren't right to bring Nemesis into play.

Across the wall, the knights were pushing and cursing. They were fighting hard, but they were tiring. Their heavy hauberks and mail leggings were beginning to drag, and they were starting to suffer from the poor ventilation of their barrel helms. Enormously strong as they were, they were not accustomed to fighting afoot, much less to trudging uphill against an entrenched enemy.

The defense began to weaken as the inexorable wall of shields pushed the spearpoints back to the wall. The knights were regaining their mad vigor as they saw their enemy weakening. Falcon gauged their mood to a remarkable fineness, then he raised his horn and sounded two short blasts.

The attacking knights did not notice when the first boulders began bounding among them. Then the big rocks were leaping through the tight formation, knocking men over like the wooden pins villagers used in their bowling games.

De Beaumont looked about him to determine the origin of this unorthodox attack. The stones were being tumbled down the hillsides, tumbling from above the ceiling of fog. With a clawing dread, he knew the feeling of defeat. Many a Western leader would have fallen into a despairing flight, but the Archbishop de Beaumont had learned the art of true war in Outremer, where a defeat in the field was only a temporary setback. "Break off!" he shouted. "Pick up our wounded and ride for the castle!" He ranged among the men, clouting helms and pushing his men to their mounts. Marco caught on quickly and did likewise. "This place is not for us!" de Beaumont shouted. "We'll take care of these louts later. Our Master is testing us! To horse, and ride for the fort. We'll defeat them there!"

The defenders gaped. They could not believe that their enemies had fled, but those were the retreating rumps of horses, and the mounts bore riders. They began a ragged cheering. Lilitha and her women came running down out of the mist. The Old Woman threw her arms around Falcon's neck.

"You've done it, Draco!" she said. "You've defeated them! Now we're safe!" Gently, Falcon disengaged her arms.

"We've not defeated them, love," Falcon said. "We've barely even tested their strength." She looked at him quizzically. "They aren't defeated?" she said, mystified.

"No," Falcon said. "This was a test of strength. This time, I tricked them into fighting on ground favorable to us. Now de Beaumont will try to bring us to his castle, where the odds are all on his side. We've hurt them, but not all that greatly. They still number more than twice the strength of my army."

Lilitha looked at him, mystified. "They're not defeated? But they've run!"

"That's not the same thing as being defeated, my love," Falcon said, "and de Beaumont knows it well. Now we'll have to besiege them."

"How do we do that?" Lilitha asked. "We have to get the flocks to pasture or they'll die. The fields need tending. The cows have to be milked or they'll sicken."

Falcon sighed. Like the others, she was so rooted in the realities of life that the practices of war seemed trivial to her. "Don't worry, love," he said. "We'll finish them before long, or you'll have no need to worry about your fields and flocks, one way or the other."

Falcon took up the pursuit at the head of his men, as was his usual practice. He mounted one of the horses they had seized from the black riders and rode toward the castle, heedless of the fact that he was separating himself from his men. The fog closed in around him. He knew the way, but the mist was disorienting.

Suddenly, a horse loomed up out of the fog, barreling into his own. Falcon's horse whinnied and went sprawling, and its rider leaped free of the saddle, snatching Nemesis from her sheath. The misty figure loomed above him, trying to bring his beast under control.

"Ye shitbrained pukelouse!" shouted the other rider. "Out of me fucking way, or I'll ride ye down like the dragon turd ye are!"

"Rupert!" Falcon shouted, his joy abated only by the necessity of staying alive against the man's assault. "It's me, Draco!"

"Eh, what's that you say, ye pus-licker?" Rupert demanded, waving his huge wooden hammer menacingly. Falcon stayed well clear, for he knew the weapon to be, in Rupert's hands, far deadlier than any conventional arm wielded by an ordinary knight.

"It's Draco, you wine-soaked old fart! Put that maul down!"

"Lord Draco, is it?" Rupert said. He whooped and jumped from his horse and gathered his leader into his arms. "I've been riding ahead of the lads, knowing my lord would be in the thick of things, far beyond the help of those turd-brains!"

Falcon endured the winy embrace. Rupert Foul-Mouth was his most valued vassal. The old man had been a woodworker in his youth, and was now a siege engineer so valuable that he was worth his triple pay and the endurance of his eccentricities. "Let go, you ancient winesack!" Falcon said. "Where are the men?"

"Not far behind," Rupert said. "That chivalrous little prig, Ruy, he has them in hand." Rupert turned sober for a change. "Now, m'lord, where be yer enemies and what must we do?"

Falcon could have wept for gratitude to have his band back with him. "About two hours' ride up this path is a fort. Simon's told you what it's like, I take it?"

"That he did," Rupert said. The one-eyed man's profane manner dropped away for a moment. "He says the wall's not too high, so I had ladders made that'll top 'em and not weigh too heavy. From the way he described the ground, towers'll be useless, so I left 'em behind. I got some good hair rope from that Savoyard we were working for, so we've got the makings for good torsion catapults."

"That's excellent!" Falcon said. Next to iron, good cordage was probably the most difficult thing to come by when men were waging war. Torsion catapults needed bundles of twisted rope, and ropes made of twisted hair, animal or human, were the best. Trebuchets, catapults that used falling weight for their motive power, were easy to make, but they were high-trajectory weapons. Torsion catapults could aim their fire directly at the tops of walls.

"Come on, Rupert," Falcon said, "they're getting away. Let's catch them." He made a move toward his horse, but Rupert's hand upon his shoulder pulled him up short.

"Hold on there, m'lord," the old man said. His grip was as powerful as one of his war machines. "Them buggers is well ahead of us. Let 'em hole up in their warren.

We'll make a proper siege of it and we'll winkle 'em out just like an abbess a-prongin' the novices."

Falcon sat down, suddenly aware of his fatigue. "You're right, Rupert," he said. "We'll besiege them as soon as the sun rises. What about those Crusaders that the lowland baron is assembling?"

"That I wouldn't know, my lord," Rupert said. "Ye'd better ask Simon." Falcon hoped that the Crusaders were far behind. It would be pointless to save these people from de Beaumont's madmen only to have them wiped out in the name of Christ. He sat down on the ground and waited for his men.

ELEVEN

FALCON surveyed the enemy fortifications. Over the gate, a line of the black helms were visible above the edge of the stockade. For the first time since entering the mountains, Falcon felt in total control of his situation. The siege engines were being assembled. The ground was too steep for anything except catapults and ladders. The Welshmen and the Genoese crossbowmen were in position. Wulf and Donal were directing Rupert's hammermen in digging-in positions among the crags above the old abbey.

Once, Falcon saw de Beaumont surveying the besiegers from his wall. The Black Pope was in armor, but only his mail coif covered his head. His face was grim and had lost its customary mask of joviality. Falcon had smiled to see the change. At his side Guido had raised his crossbow for a shot, but Falcon stayed him. "Not that one, Guido. He's mine." The Genoese had shrugged and tried a shot at a man standing to de Beaumont's right. The range was long and there was a stiff breeze blowing, so he scored a near miss.

Ruy Ortiz came striding up, resplendent in new armor.

He had appropriated a black riders' hauberk and leggings, and had removed the blackening by rolling them in a barrel full of gravel, sand, and vinegar. Now they shone bright as silver. "The men are ready for the assault, Sir Draco," he said.

"Good. What did you do with your old hauberk?"

"I've given it to my squire. It's time he had man's armor."

"I'm not sure I like those leggings," Falcon said.

"I'll try them for a while to see if they're worth their weight. They're very handsome, though, don't you think?" Ruy stuck out a leg and turned it, admiring the sheen of the mail.

Falcon sighed. Ruy was always the first to adopt any new foolery demanded by the cult of chivalry. "The ladies will love them, Ruy. I don't want to catch you with one of those iron pots over your head, though."

"I don't care for them either, my lord," Ruy said. "Now, shall I order the ladder parties forward?"

"Do so," Falcon said.

"Sir," Ruy said, "may I have the honor of leading the assault?"

"Hmm," Falcon mused. "Who got to go first last time?"

"Rudolph of Austria. And the time before that it was the new man, Sir Andrew."

"Oh, very well, then, lead the first team."

"Thank you, my lord!" said Ruy, beaming. Falcon turned away, shaking his head. It was like this every time. All of the knights and squires vied with one another to be the first atop the wall, as if it made any difference to the outcome of the battle. Personal honor was all they cared for. It was as if, to them, real life in some way resembled those poems they were so fond of. Well, he had been like that too, years ago.

They would attack on a narrow front, concentrating on

the gates and the wall flanking them. Falcon knew that there were stairs leading down into the courtyard near the gates, so it would not be necessary to fight their way to a stair once they had gained the wall. Ordinarily, Falcon tried to avoid such concentration of his forces, but here it didn't matter, because de Beaumont had no missile troops. The most his men could do was to throw down rocks or spears. They had no supply of pitch or oil or lead to heat and pour down upon the attackers. Guido would be directing Falcon's own archers and crossbowmen from the crags above the fort, firing directly into the backs of the defenders.

If the assault was to be simple, the fighting atop the wall was another matter. De Beaumont had no rabble of untrained and ill-armed villeins to defend his fort. Every man was a knight trained to arms from birth. Each was protected by splendid armor and armed with the best weapons to be had. All would fight with unnatural ferocity, even for men who faced certain death if they were defeated. Falcon was expecting severe casualties from this fight. To make things worse, this was a personal matter, not business. It wasn't fair to the men, and he hoped that de Beaumont had sufficient loot heaped in his treasury to satisfy them. An ordinary baron would have no compunction about sacrificing the lives of all his men to satisfy his own honor, but Falcon was a professional soldier, not a military landlord.

Wulf walked up to him, yellow hair streaming out from under his steel cap. "Ready to go, my lord?"

Falcon picked up his shield and tossed his head around a few times to assure himself that his helmet was tied down snugly. He took his ax from his belt and unclipped the leather sheath that protected its edge. He always preferred the ax for ladder assaults. "Ready," he said.

There were four ladders, each under the command of a knight. Ruy Ortiz had one, and Sir Randolph of Austria another. The other two were commanded by Sir Andrew and by Falcon himself. Sir Andrew was a Scot and had joined the band only a few months before. He fought on foot with an odd combination weapon: It was a long-handled poleax, and on the side opposite the ax blade was a sharp, downcurving hook. At its top was a spear point. With this vicious weapon, Sir Andrew could chop, hook, and stab, as well as clout or trip his foes with its long shaft. Normally, Falcon was dubious of weapons designed to perform more than one function, but Sir Andrew had demonstrated his deadliness with the thing, which he had named Maid's Kiss.

As Falcon's men drew close to the wall, the black knights set up their unearthly howling, and Falcon could see some of his own men beginning to falter a little at this pack of seemingly demonic enemies. He was about to harangue them when Sir Ruy made it unnecessary.

"They're only men!" the Spanish knight shouted. "They die when you open them up! Now put that ladder against the wall and get out of my way!" Falcon grinned. Ortiz wasn't very bright, but he was as brave as any man Falcon had ever known. With his shield held high before him, Sir Ruy began trudging his way up the ladder. Big stones crashed into the shield, but the tough construction of wood faced with leather and rimmed and studded with iron was proof against them. By the time Ruy was half-way up the ladder, two others were in place, and the knights Rudolph and Andrew were on their way up. Falcon held his own ladder in reserve while he observed the progress of the assault.

"Sir Ruy will be regretting those iron stockings about now," said Wulf. It was plain that the Spanish knight was making heavy going of the climb. Even so, it was clear that he would make it. Wulf and Falcon had seen knights more heavy-laden climbing ladders five times as long to scale the monster fortifications of Palestine, and doing it under a scorching sun.

"Where'll we put the ladder?" Wulf asked.

"Take the right flank, next to Andrew's," Falcon ordered. "They're hard pressed there." Even as he spoke, he saw Sir Andrew's ladder topple, but the Scot jumped well clear of it in time and sprang up uninjured. Immediately, he was ordering his men to replace the ladder and try again.

Falcon's men got his ladder wedged firmly against the wall, and he took his place, as was customary, at the head of the ascending line. From the ladder next to him, Sir Andrew was grinning across the intervening distance. "They fight hard, my lord." At that instant, a fist-sized rock clanged from Andrew's helmet.

"Keep your shield up!" Falcon ordered. His left arm was beginning to ache from holding his own shield against the rain of stones from above. Atop the wall, men with forked poles were striving to push the ladders away, but the narrowness of the wallwalk did not allow them to get much weight behind the poles, while below Rupert's men were bracing the ladders with timbers and blocks of stone.

There came a new sound from above, and Falcon saw an object hurtle past that was not a stone. It was a black pot helm, and there was a head inside it. "Ruy's gained the wall!" he shouted, and he redoubled his efforts. Even a fighter as fierce as Ruy Ortiz could not hold out alone for more than a few minutes. It was imperative that they take advantage of the confusion he was creating before he was cut down.

Above the rim of his shield, Falcon could see black helms, and now they were within ax range. His ax flashed out, and he saw a helm fall away in two pieces. A sword cracked into the edge of his shield, and he crushed its wielder's shoulder, and then, for half a second, the wall beyond his ladder was clear. Half a second was all he needed. With a bellow, Falcon was over the wall and on the wallwalk, striving to keep his feet under him in the litter of bodies and blood and weapons. Wulf scrambled up behind him, and they rushed to meet the nearest enemies. The knights fought hard and skillfully, but Falcon's attack was like some deadly natural force, and within minutes his men were pouring onto the wall from all four ladders.

De Beaumont stared at the men coming over his wall in utter disbelief. How could it happen? His men were invincible! How had he failed? His Master could not have deserted him. Had he failed to interpret the spells correctly? Had he made some mistake in performing the rituals? Everything had gone perfectly, just as promised, until Draco de Montfalcon had sprung up from nowhere, seemingly returned from the dead. Maybe that was it. Yes, it had to be. Draco was much more than he pretended to be. He was possessed of great magic. The others must be warned, so that the Master's will could be carried out. He rushed to his chamber and opened his chest. From it he removed his most precious books and papers, the ones he would most need to carry on his work elsewhere. He also took a heavy sack of gold coins. He stowed his treasures in a pair of saddlebags and slung them across his shoulder. With his club in his hand, he went out onto the gallery and made his way toward the chapel.

Falcon's men were in the courtyard now. This relatively open space favored the defending knights, and the battle had entered a stage of incredible ferocity. Behind locked shields, the knights were slowly giving ground. Falcon's missile troops had come back down from the crags and had taken up positions on the wallwalk, from which they were calmly firing at short range into the packed mass of knights. Every crossbow bolt and arrow dropped a man.

A sword-and-buckler fighter tried to block de Beaumont's way, only to be smashed against the wall by the terrible club. De Beaumont stepped over the quivering body and gained the doorway to the chapel. Dashing inside, he threw the bolts. He crossed the room to stand before the goat-headed idol on the pedestal behind the blood-soaked altar. Hands clasped before him, de Beaumont bowed deeply.

"Forgive me, Master. I have failed you, although I do not understand how. Aid me to rejoin the other Brethren, and I shall strive to do your bidding with even greater zeal."

Unceremoniously, de Beaumont pushed at the shoulder of the idol. Slowly, idol and pedestal slid aside to reveal a square hole in the floor. De Beaumont dropped his saddlebags through and then struggled to squeeze his armored bulk through the small opening. He dropped a few feet to the dank stone floor beneath. This tunnel had been a drainage channel from the old bathhouse used when this had been a legionary fort. De Beaumont had discovered it during his restorations and had incorporated it into his defenses as an escape route. He had never expected the place to be besieged, much less taken, but it was almost instinctive to have a sally port or a covered passage included among a castle's attributes.

Draco Falcon axed the man before him and hewed at another before the first fell. From the dynamic assault, the fight had degenerated into the kind of static battle seldom seen anymore. Both armies now stretched the width of the courtyard and faced one another over a wall of overlapping shields. It had turned into a battle of attrition; long, bloody and exhausting. Falcon's men were gradually gaining ground, though. They were more experienced at foot fighting, and the archers were still picking off men among the black ranks.

Falcon had been fighting ceaselessly since mounting the ladder. His endurance was great, but his arm was beginning to tire, the ax getting heavier with each stroke. His defense with his shield was slowing, and now his nose was bleeding from a mace blow he'd taken on the helmet. The fine Saracen steel had deflected most of the blow's force, but his ears were still ringing.

"Get back, my lord," said Sir Rudolph of Austria. The Austrian knight was fighting on Falcon's right. "I'll cover you while you step back. You're getting too tired to fight. Go get some wine and rest awhile, then come back. You're not doing any good now." Falcon nodded. The man was right. Disengaging from a battle was always a tricky business. He stepped back while Rudolph skillfully maneuvered his shield to cover him and prevent an exploitable gap from appearing in the line. Another man adroitly stepped around Falcon and took his place in the front of the battle line.

Falcon stumbled wearily back to the base of the wall, where Rupert Foul-Mouth handed him a skin of wine. Unfastening his aventail, Falcon raised the skin and directed a stream of the amber liquid into his mouth.

"Going pretty well, my lord," Rupert said. "Not much work for me, though." The old man sounded disappointed.

"We've lost too many, Rupert," Falcon said bitterly. "Too many just to take a little mountain fort from a pack of madmen."

"Well," Rupert shrugged philosophically, "men die anyway, and there's not much to be done about it. We've both seen armies lose half their strength to sickness just sitting around camp. Besides," he went on, rubbing his horny palms together greedily, producing a sound like two wood rasps mating, "the way these ape turds've been scouring in the lowlands, there's probably plenty of good pickings in this place!" The old man chuckled at the prospect.

Gradually, the noise across the courtyard abated. Ruy

Ortiz, his fine new mail now crimson, his shield slashed and splintered, came to stand before Falcon. He was gasping, and he took a moment to shake the clotted blood from Moorslayer and catch his breath. "The enemy ask for quarter, my lord" he said when he had breath.

Falcon looked across the yard. It was usually his custom to grant quarter to his enemies who laid down their arms and asked it when they saw that further resistance was useless. That was in an ordinary battle, against other soldiers. He scanned the remaining foe, their armor now so dusty and bloody that they would have been hard to distinguish from his own men, had it not been for their grotesque helms. He could see that de Beaumont was not among them. He thought of the slaughtered village he'd seen, of the boy on the altar here in the chapel, just a few days ago.

"No quarter," Falcon said.

Without pity he heard the screams of the last of the Black Army. He was intent on more important business. With Nemesis in his fist, he went to de Beaumont's chamber. He saw in an instant that his enemy wasn't there, but he paused to scan the contents of the chest. The most important documents were gone, and that meant that de Beaumont had a way out.

Frantic now, Falcon set every man who could walk to the search for de Beaumont. Within minutes, he was called to the chapel. He cursed loudly when he saw the tunnel, then he dropped into it heedlessly, with Wulf and the others at his heels, and raced down the black passageway as if he could find his way in the dark like a bat.

The passage emerged from a hillside well below and to the rear of the fortress. There was a small meadow in which a few horses grazed. Raging and fuming, Falcon called for his swiftest horse.

"We'll never catch him, my lord," Wulf said. "He has too long a head start on us."

"I can catch him!" Falcon shouted. "The bastard weighs three hundred pounds and he's armored, so he can't ride fast. Get my fastest courser and I'll catch him."

De Beaumont's tracks led uphill, away from the fort. They were easy to follow in the soft spring grass, but it was also clear that he had taken several horses. It was not long before Falcon passed one of them, dead of exhaustion. He cursed. Could he make it? Even changing horses, de Beaumont had to take the time to stop and change his saddle to another steed.

Falcon came to a slope that slanted downward to a deep, narrow gorge. From the depths of the gorge he could hear the rumble of swift waters. De Beaumont was riding toward the gorge. Then Falcon saw the bridge. It was a narrow plank roadway slung from ropes attached to stone posts on either side of the cleft. De Beaumont was almost up to it.

Falcon spurred his horse mercilessly down the slope, heedless of the risk he was taking. It did not seem possible that the flimsy bridge could take the weight of the fat archbishop, his huge horse and his armor and packs, but it held. Falcon was still two furlongs from the bridge when de Beaumont dismounted on the far side. He saw the ax in the man's hands and let forth a groan of despair. De Beaumont began hewing at the supporting cables, and Falcon made a last mad rush to cross the bridge before it fell.

As the bridge began to topple, Falcon made no move to check his horse's pace. He headed toward de Beaumont at a full gallop, as if he expected to cross the chasm by force of willpower alone. Fortunately, the horse was not so foolhardy. It sat back on its haunches and skidded through the damp grass. Falcon went flying over its head and rolled to the very edge of the gorge, coming to a halt against a stone, temporarily rendered unconscious.

When Wulf and the others caught up with him, he was

kneeling on the ground and facing the bridge as if he could wish it back into existence. With both fists he was pounding the ground and raving wordlessly. Wulf signaled for the others to stay back, then he rode up to dismount by his master.

"I lost him, Wulf," he said. "I had him in my hands and I lost him." He turned to look at Wulf. The whites of his eyes had gone blood-red. There were traces of drying foam at the corners of his mouth.

Ruy Ortiz began to ride forward to his master's aid, but Donal MacFergus stopped him. "I've seen him like this before, Ruy. He'll kill you if you get too close. Give Wulf time to calm him."

"How did he do it, Wulf?" Falcon was not raging now, but Wulf knew from his eyes and his stance and the way his whole body trembled that Falcon was not yet in his right mind. "Does that filthy god of his really protect him? I must have him, Wulf. I'll sell my soul."

"Now, Draco," Wulf said soothingly. "We've let enemies get away before."

"Never one of *them*!" Falcon shouted.

"But we've broken his power."

"Don't you see, Wulf? He'll warn the others! Now they'll all know that I'm alive and that I'm looking for them. How can I have my vengeance now? How can I die satisfied that I can face my father again?" He was beginning to foam again.

"Think of it this way, Draco: Maybe now they'll come looking for you."

For a long moment Falcon stared at Wulf uncomprehendingly. Then his eyes began to clear a little, and the trembling quieted. "Yes, you're right," he said at last. "That would save us a good deal of time, wouldn't it? Maybe they'll all come at once." Now Falcon was actually smiling. He shook himself and looked around, noticing his band of men for the first time. "When did they get here?"

He spotted the one-eyed old man astride a bay horse. "Rupert, come over here!" The others vented a collective sigh of relief to see their master sound again.

"Aye, my lord?" Rupert said.

Falcon pointed at the standing bridge supports. "How long will it take you to bridge that gap strongly enough for the army to cross?"

Rupert squinted at the chasm and the standing stones. "Won't be easy. The timbers I have are too short, but I've plenty of rope. Have to get some men to the other side, though." He turned the intriguing problem over in his mind. "Give me a week, my lord."

"You have it," Falcon said.

"Surely you don't intend to follow de Beaumont after he's had a week's head start?" said Wulf.

"No, I just want a way out of these mountains."

"Uh, my lord," Wulf said, not sure that Falcon was quite recovered yet, "there's a perfectly good path out of here—the one we took coming in. And it'll be a lot safer than any bridge across this gorge."

"My bridge'll be safe, ye tit-sucking puppy!" Rupert said, brindling at the implied insult to his engineering skill.

"I don't want to leave the way we came," Falcon said. "I have a plan for dealing with those Crusaders from the lowland. Come on, let's go back to the fort and see what we've won."

The chests had been opened and the loot piled in the courtyard. The haul was rich: Gold and silver church plate, crucifixes and relics, tapestries, rich fabrics and furs, spices, reliquaries, preserved foods, fine arms and armor. Besides the material goods, there was a splendid store of livestock; more than four hundred horses, many of them trained warhorses, as well as cattle, sheep, and pigs remaining from the black riders' last raid.

"Fresh meat for a good while, my lord," reported Simon the Monk, who was Falcon's steward. He was the only man besides Falcon himself who could read and write. "And marching rations for weeks. The goods we can sell or divide among the men now."

"We'll wait and sell them later," Falcon said. He disliked dividing loot in bulk. It always led to arguments and fights among the men. He much preferred to sell loot and divide the money fairly. The problem was that coinage was always in short supply. Even kings had trouble getting their hands on minted money and usually ended up paying their men in chickens or cheeses or bolts of cloth.

"With all these mounts and these arms and armor, we can equip a much larger force of knights and sergeants," Ruy Ortiz noted. Sergeants were men armed and mounted as knights who lacked the lineage and family ties for sponsorship into knighthood. The Spanish knight's eyes glowed at the prospect of a bigger cavalry arm.

"Since we can mount and equip them," Falcon mused, "we can accept men who've been impoverished by ransom, or returned Crusaders who fell ill and had to sell their gear." The idea appealed to him. By ancient tradition, the bestowal of arms bound a vassal to his lord even more strongly than the taking of service and the oath of fealty.

Simon was looking into a silken bag. "What's this stuff?" he asked. Falcon took the bag. Inside it was a mixture of herbs. He sniffed it. It was the drug mixture used in the Black Army's rites. Falcon smiled.

"This is going to come in handy," he announced. "Simon, I have a task for you."

The baron surveyed his men with some satisfaction. They were mostly his own dependents, along with a sprinkling of professionals who were along for the adventure and the loot. All wore new white surcoats stitched with crosses to signify their holy mission. There was a great rabble of commoners to see to the needs of their betters and a gathering of camp followers and whores to keep them tended and entertained along the way. All had received communion and absolution that morning.

The baron was proud of his accomplishment. In a mere two months, he had assembled this force and marched it the full thirty miles to the mouth of the gorge from which the demonic riders had emerged so many times. Before them marched a band of priests and acolytes bearing crucifixes, swinging censers, and chanting.

He looked forward to the coming battle. They would have a fine summer: first take care of the black riders, then slaughter the mountain heathen, winkling them out of their hiding places and cutting them down, men, women, and children. It would be good sport, profitable activity, and it was sanctioned by the church, so everyone's soul would be the better for it. Besides, there hadn't been a war with his neighbors in two years and the hunting in his forests had been very poor of late.

The baron was about to order his army up the gorge with a hearty "God wills it!" when there came a hideous scream from the narrow, misty path. A figure in monastic garments came running and stumbling along the path, howling like a lost soul. They all gaped as the creature approached. What new horror had the mountain valley spawned?

The man emerged into the light. He seemed to be a monk. He wore a belted brown robe with a cowl, and he was barefoot and his crown was shaved in a tonsure. It was his face, though, that sent the nearest men recoiling back in horror. It was flushed bright red and sweating profusely though the morning was cool. It was covered all over with black blotches, as were the man's hands, scalp, and feet. There could be no question that the man bore some horrible disease.

"Go back!" the apparition shouted. "Go back, my brethren! God has stricken the valley! He has smitten the unholy riders with the Egyptian pox! He has afflicted the heathen with a foul murrain, with the black vomit and the bloody flux of the bowels! Flee the place of God's wrath or you will be consumed by worms and maggots!" The monk grabbed his throat with both hands and spun around three or four times. "Aaaaaarrrgh!" he bellowed, then he flopped to his back and lay with his heels drumming on the earth. After several minutes of this he lay still.

The assembled army stood gaping in silence; then, as one man, they turned and fled. At their forefront rode the baron, fuming and terrified. He'd spent half his treasury assembling this force in anticipation of good loot. Now what was he going to do to recoup his losses? He fell to pondering which of his neighbors stood in need of a good raid.

When even the last of the camp followers was out of sight, Simon got up and brushed himself off. Down the gorge came Falcon, Wulf, and Donal, their laughter echoing off the sides of the gorge, tears streaming down their faces.

"How did I do, my lord?" Simon asked.

"I'm almost afraid to go near you," Falcon said. He tossed his man a towel, and Simon rubbed off the blotches of soot and dried blood with which his skin had been decorated. He retained the red coloration.

"Good thing I'm not armed," Simon said, his breath still coming heavily. "I was seeing demons all the way down the path. I think I'd've taken on that whole army if I'd had my morningstar. What's in that drug?"

"I've no idea," Falcon said. "And now I've made use of it, I'm going to dump it in the river."

Still chuckling, the men headed up the path to their tethered horses.

"Oh, Draco, Draco!" Lilitha's legs were wrapped around his waist, striving to pull him into her even more deeply. Her fingers dug into his shoulders as she pushed him up to arm's length. Her head was back, mouth open and gasping as if she could never get enough air. Falcon drove himself with all the coiled power of his muscles and heart. His sweat rained down upon her as hers soaked the pallet beneath her writhing body. Then everything inside him seemed to liquefy and it was as if his very soul were pouring up into her.

She felt it and drew him down, covering his mouth with hers and sucking in his breath as he trembled and climaxed in one final powerful surge. Slowly their wrenching embrace loosened. They rolled to their sides and fell away from one another, needing to cool their overheated bodies. Lilitha's legs still held him loosely, and he was still within her, as he had been for the last three hours.

Falcon ran his hand down her shoulder and over her sweat-slicked breast. Her nipples were gradually subsiding from their former rocklike hardness. So ardent had been their lovemaking that their bodies steamed faintly in the cool predawn air. Her lips were swollen and her cheeks flushed in the dim firelight, and she looked ten years younger than her age. Falcon was first to break the silence.

"Come with me, Lilitha," he said at last.

"Not now, my love," she said. "We will talk about it later." Her eyes were still closed, and her lashes lay upon her cheeks as delicately as the wings of black butterflies.

"No, give me your answer now," Falcon demanded. "We ride with the first light. I must know."

Slowly, reluctantly, she pulled away from him. There was a faint, damp sound as he slid from her body. She sat on the pallet, drawing her knees up to her chin and hugging her thighs against her breasts. "Very well," she said at length. "No, Draco, I cannot go with you."

"But why?" he asked. "You would be my wife. You want children, don't you? I'll give you a houseful. In time, I'll make you a great lady, with castles and lands and servants. I'll have poets to sing of your beauty."

"And what would I be in your world, Draco? Just an ignorant country woman from a place nobody ever heard of. I know nothing of castles and estates. I want your children, but I don't wish to raise them in a place where men slaughter one another for profit or honor or vengeance.

"Here, I am the Old Woman. I am loved and respected and honored. I want my daughter to be Old Woman after me. My people need me and I need them. I couldn't go to a place where I would never hear my own tongue spoken again. All here are my kin. I know their families as well as my own. I would wither and die away from these mountains." She looked at him with a great sadness.

"Ask yourself this, Draco: Would you give up your warrior's life and your vengeance, your men and your wandering, to live the rest of your life here with me?"

"You know I cannot," he said, her words like nails in his heart.

"Then," she said, "let's leave the future until tomorrow. We still have two hours until dawn." Then he was drunk again with the rich smell of her and he bore her in his arms to the pallet and sank into her once more, for the last time.

Rupert's bridge stretched across the narrow chasm, much more solid-looking than the old one had been. The heavy wagons were already across and the construction had barely shaken. Falcon remained behind to make his final farewells. A group of villagers had come to see them off. There was not a sorrowful face among them. Falcon was expecting that. A soldier grew accustomed to tearless leavetakings. Nobody was ever sorry to see soldiers depart.

"My people thank you, Draco," Lilitha said.

"They're happy to see the last of us, though," Falcon observed.

"That does not mean they are not grateful. But they are farmers and herders, and they concern themselves with the things of life. You and your men are killers." She said this without rancor or judgment. "Your kind and ours cannot live together for long."

"I suppose you're right," Falcon said. "I hope I've given you what you wanted."

"You have," she said, smiling.

"Are you sure?" he asked, grinning hugely.

"I know. There are ways."

"I hope it's a son, to grow tall and strong to protect you in your old age."

"I'm hoping for a daughter, to follow me as Old Woman."

"Maybe we'll be lucky and it'll be one of each." He fumbled with his reins. "Farewell, Lilitha." She raised a hand wordlessly, then let it fall to her side.

"Farewell."

Falcon wheeled his horse and rode across the bridge. He went to the head of his column and joined Wulf.

"Where do we ride, my lord?" Wulf asked. Falcon turned a grim face to him.

"Who cares?" he said.

The following is an action-packed excerpt from
the next novel in this sword-swinging new Signet
series set in the age of chivalry:
THE FALCON 3:   THE BLOODY CROSS

ONE

THE road heading toward Paris was muddy. But
then, it was fall, and roads leading everywhere were
muddy. The two riders cursed the mud, the rain, the slow
pace of their mounts, and anything else that occurred to
them.

"My mail's going to rust," said the younger rider. He
wore a steel cap, beneath which hung a curtain of tangled
yellow hair.

"Roll it up and stow it in an oiled bag, as I did with
mine," said the elder. He was a striking man, tall and
lean, with a blaze of white hair running in a streak
through his otherwise coal-black locks.

"And ride unprotected through strange territory?" said
the yellow-haired man. "You can pamper that fine
Saracen gear of yours if you like, but I'm willing to put

up with a little rust." He scanned the dripping trees. "That inn has to be somewhere near."

"Why?" grumbled the other. " 'About two hours from here,' that peasant said. Two hours for what? A horse? A man? A peasant carrying a load of firewood?"

"If he was talking about two hours for an eagle, we're in trouble," the younger man said.

They rounded a bend. A short distance from them they could see a crossroads, and at the crossroads was a collection of low, rambling buildings. There were sheds and stables and a courtyard, all surrounded by a timber stockade. "The inn!" both men shouted at once. They kicked their horses into a trot.

As they rode up, they could see a cheery light coming from under the thatched eaves. They had been riding all day, and they dismounted somewhat stiffly. A boy came to take their horses, and they picked up their bags and went inside.

The innkeeper met them at the door. "Come in, sirs, and good day to you. You look hungry and cold and wet. Please make yourselves comfortable by the fire while I send for some refreshment for you. How shall I announce you?" The men gave their names and followed the man into a low-beamed, smoky room. Gathered around a hearth were about twenty people from all stations in life. Some were eating and all were drinking wine or ale.

The innkeeper said, importantly: "My lords and ladies and others, I present Sir Draco Falcon and his man, Wulf." Those gathered made a place for the men near the fire and scanned him surreptitiously. Falcon was a tall man with handsome, hawklike features. His face was burned deep brown, bisected by a thin white line that began at his hairline at the base of the white streak and ran down through his eyebrow, down the cheek and jaw and neck to disappear beneath his tunic. The eyebrow was white where the line crossed it. The men and the women present sized him up and both were impressed with what they saw, though for different reasons.

A man handed Falcon a cup of hot spiced wine. "I am Philippe de Chambord, Sir Draco. I am master of the vintners' guild of Paris." Philippe wore clothing that was rich though travel-stained. The vintners' guild stood high in the royal favor. "We've just been discussing the latest news. Have you heard about Richard Lion-Heart of England?"

"Richard? No, I haven't heard about him in months."

"He's dead," said a man past middle age, attired as a knight. "The light of chivalry is dead at the siege of Chaluz."

"Dead?" Falcon said. It saddened him. He had hoped to kill Richard himself, someday. "How? And where is Chaluz?"

"It's a castle belonging to the Viscount of Limoges," the old knight said. "He and Richard were embroiled in some petty affray over a treasure trove. They say that a crossbowman shot Richard in the neck. The wound was not serious, but it festered and he died."

"A crossbowman? Richard? How fitting!" Falcon could not help chuckling, though some of those present were scandalized. It was known throughout Christendom that Richard had shocked the world by wielding a crossbow in the Crusade. The weapon had been forbidden for use against Christians, but the Pope had declared it lawful for killing heathens. Still, the sight of a king using a weapon relegated to the lowest of footmen had shaken the world of chivalry.

Falcon removed his sword belt and seated himself on a stool, keeping the sword propped between his knees. It was long and curved, clearly not of European origin. Its guard was a large bronze crescent and its grip was long enough for two hands. The pommel was a smaller crescent. The innkeeper's servants brought him a platter of bread and cheeses and sausages, and he began to eat ravenously.

"Sir Draco," said a lady seated nearby, "may I refill your cup?" The lady stood and brought him a pitcher of wine. He placed her accent somewhere near the Rhine. She was unusually tall, close to six feet, and her tight-fitting gown revealed that she was built with a Junoesque lushness. Her coif and wimple hid her hair, but her eyebrows were so white as to be nearly invisible. Her features were large, regular, and handsome rather than conventionally beautiful. "I am Lady Gudrun von Kleist. I am returning from a pilgrimage to Rome."

"By way of Paris?" Falcon asked.

"I've always wanted to see Paris," Lady Gudrun said. Whatever for?, Falcon wondered.

"Do you travel alone or in company?" Falcon asked. Ordinarily pilgrims were safe upon the roads, even women on pilgrimage alone, but the times were troubled and many brigands and robber barons regarded even pilgrims as fair game.

"I have my ladies with me, and a cook and groom, and a few pages and such. Aside from these, I am alone." It was clear that Lady Gudrun regarded herself as in company only with persons of her own rank. "Oh," she continued, "there is also Fra Benedetto." She gestured toward a seated man who wore the habit of a friar. Within his raised cowl, the obscured head bowed slightly. Falcon bowed slightly in return. Very slightly. He was not fond of the church, nor of its minions. At an early age, his boyish religious enthusiasms had been washed away in the bloodbaths of the Crusades. Once upon a time, he had been shocked deeply at the corruption and venality of the church. Now he was not even amused.

Fra Benedetto was attired as a Franciscan, but his habit, while of that order's plain design and cut, was of fine cloth. The man raised delicate white hands and pushed the cowl back, to reveal a face small-boned and slightly vulpine. He smiled with thin lips. "Good evening, Sir Draco," he said. He spoke Provençal but his accent was thick Italian.

"Fra Benedetto," Lady Gudrun said, "has been kind enough to accompany us since we left Rome." Her expression and tone said that this kindness had been unwanted and unasked for. "Sir Draco, I take it that Paris is your destination also?"

"It is, my lady."

"How wonderful! Will you consent to ride with us? With the roads so dangerous in these disgraceful times, the presence of armed men such as you and your squire would be a great comfort."

Falcon groaned inwardly. He had been fearing this. He hated to travel with a pack of straggling foot travelers. He had been hoping to reach Paris within two days. Now he would be lucky to make it in six. There was no help for it, though. A knight was required to supply protection if asked by a lady of high birth.

"I am, of course, at my lady's disposal," Falcon said. Almost unconsciously, he had slipped into the courtly French of castle and palace. Ordinarily, he spoke the rough soldier's patois of the camps.

"Then I am sure we shall travel in safety," Lady Gudrun said, "with so chivalrous a gentleman riding before us." Falcon had little use for the artificial conventions of chivalry, but there was no escaping them. Within a generation, the vague rules of conduct for warriors concocted by crusaders, poets, and priests had become the international rage of the military aristocracy. It had been further embroidered by court ladies weary of living with armored brutes of husbands until it was something as unreal as a fairy tale.

A sudden thought struck Falcon as he brooded in his wine cup. "My God!" he exclaimed.

"What is it, sir?" asked the vintner.

"If Richard's dead, that means John Lackland is king of England. If King Philip wants to take England, there will never be a better time." This remark caused a babble of comment. Falcon's mind worked furiously. If King Philip, who was now being called Augustus, wanted to invade England, he would be hiring soldiers. Falcon was captain of a band of professionals who hired their services to the highest bidder. Until now, they had been fighting petty affrays, settling squabbles between barons over land or honor. Here was the prospect of a major campaign. If Philip took England from John, every one of Falcon's men could become rich. Falcon and his wellborn officers could expect to be made major landholders.

He had other reasons to hope for a war. If King Philip called up his vassals, Odo FitzRoy would have to appear with his men. In England, Falcon would find Nigel Edgehill among the opposing forces. He had sworn a holy oath to kill these two men, and two others. One of the four he had tracked down and killed two years before. Another, the Archbishop de Beaumont, he had found, but the man had escaped. Edgehill and FitzRoy he had not seen in more than a dozen years.

"I think not, just yet," said the vintner, interrupting Falcon's reverie.

"Why do you say that?" Falcon asked.

"Philip Augustus has enough troubles at home without indulging in military adventures abroad. Richard's death is a heaven-sent opportunity to take back all the lands seized by the old king, but Philip is still deeply in debt for the funds he borrowed to mount his Crusade. My own guild alone has been owed ten thousand golden florins for more than ten years." The old king of whom the vintner spoke was Henry II of England, who had inherited, married, and conquered his way to the largest empire since the fall of Rome, most of it at the expense of the King of France. He had reduced Philip's father's holdings to a few acres of land around Paris, and Philip had spent the whole of his reign gradually reconquering his lost lands from Henry's valiant but foolish son, Richard.

"No," the vintner went on, "I think that King Philip will go on consolidating his gains, and he will be successful now that he has no Richard to stop him. He will of course demand that John come to Paris to do homage for the crown of England. John will refuse, or delay, or pretend that he didn't get the demand, or just ignore it, and things will go on like that indefinitely, as each waits for the other to die first."

As hereditary Dukes of Normandy, the Plantagenets supposedly held England in fief to the King of France, and had to renew their legitimacy with every generation by performing the oath of homage. This was legalistic fiction, for all the world knew that the Plantagenets held England by right of conquest and only needed to do homage for their French holdings, which until a few years before had included Normandy, Brittany, the Aquitaine, Angou, and a dozen minor holdings. In short, about ninety percent of France. Richard had recklessly squandered his inheritance, and now England possessed only a few holdings along the English Channel. Falcon was sure that Philip, ablest king of his line for many generations, would have those holdings back within a year.

He sighed. The vintner was probably right. It would have been a wonderful opportunity, though.

The next day, the motley band loaded up and set out for Paris. Falcon fretted impatiently as the group straggled out in the most inefficient fashion. His own little army would have been up before dawn and five miles down the road before the first of these travelers left the inn.

There were compensations to traveling with such a

group, though. Several musicians had their instruments out and were leading the band in a rousing song. A juggler was keeping six balls in the air, bouncing one off his head from time to time. A tumbler was walking along in imitation of an old man, but his pack was strapped to his belly and his staff was gripped between his toes as he walked along on his hands. Falcon could not help smiling despite his impatience.

"Is the day not beautiful?" Lady Gudrun had ridden to Falcon's side. The lowering skies of the previous day had given way to clear autumn sunlight and the puddles in the road lay steaming.

"Beautiful, indeed, my lady," Falcon acknowledged, openly admiring the German lady's graceful carriage. It was something few women could achieve riding sidesaddle. Today she wore a pink gown trimmed with ermine, so tightly fitted that Falcon could count every vertebra in her spearshaft-straight spine. He noted with interest that her large breasts bore uncommonly small nipples.

She, in turn, reciprocated his admiration. Besides his height, his handsome, aquiline features, and his striking coloration, she noted that his shoulders were wide, and that even dressed in mail his waist was as small as hers. His fine armor shimmered in the sunlight like quicksilver. The coif of mail hung down his back, to be drawn over his head at need. His conical helmet hung from his saddle next to an ax. On the other side was hung a long, kite-shaped shield. In his belt were a pair of thick gloves of black leather, their backs densely studded with small steel spikes. His soft boots were cross-gartered to the knee with strips of scarlet leather.

After a careful study of the man, masked by inconsequential small talk, her attention was drawn to the device painted on his shield. In recent years, knights had taken to painting colored designs on the faces of their shields, to make themselves recognizable in battle. The practice had grown with the adoption of helms that covered the knight's face, and now it was part of the mystique of chivalry.

Falcon's device was a bird of prey, its wings spread against a white background. In its claws were clutched bolts of blue lightning. The bird was black. On Falcon's banner the background was embroidered in silver thread, but silver gilding was too expensive for something as perishable as a shield, so white had to do.

"Oh, now I see," Lady Gudrun said. "Your name is Falcon, and that is the name of the bird in your language, isn't it?"

"Yes, it is, my lady," Falcon said, sensing a ploy. The woman spoke French fluently, though she sometimes used an awkward Germanic construction. She couldn't have spent so much time in the courts of France without learning all the terms of falconry.

"You resemble your namesake," she said, "at least in appearance. Do you also resemble it in habit?"

"Somewhat. Like the bird, I seek game to feed my dependents."

"And have you a nest somewhere?"

"Wherever my men are."

"Ah. You serve no liege, then?"

"No, my lady. I'm a free captain. I hire my services and those of my army to any who need such, and can afford them. I am bound by no oath of fealty and I have no land. Just now, my men are in winter quarters in the South."

"And what brings you to Paris, so far from your men?"

Falcon smiled. The woman was pumping him for information without giving any in return. "There is a man there who desires my services. I'm going there to meet him. And you, my lady—Paris is not the finest of cities to visit. What draws you there?"

"Oh," Gudrun said, with an airy wave of her hand, "I've been invited to the court. King Philip desires closer ties with the Graf von Kleist."

"The graf is your husband?" Falcon asked.

"Oh, no!" she said. "The graf is my son. My husband died on Crusade and is with the saints in heaven. Little Klaus is only four years old. I hope to make a good marriage for him, perhaps even one of the royal princesses."

Falcon nodded. Gudrun was in the most enviable position possible for a noble lady. As mother of the heir, she could not be displaced, and she had control of her son's estates until he attained his majority, still many years in the future. As a young and beautiful widow of good blood, she had plenty of time to negotiate an advantageous marriage for herself before handing the reins over to her son. In the meantime, she was free to travel and amuse herself on her own, something most noble women could never hope to do. Ordinarily, a noble lady was regarded as little more than a brood mare, designed for the purpose of turning out children until she was used up, and then she was shunted aside in favor of a young mistress. Gudrun would never suffer that ignominy.

Their conversation was interrupted by the arrival of Fra Benedetto. Gudrun greeted him politely, but she wore a look of annoyance. The friar was riding an extremely fine palfrey, in violation of the rules of his order and of the sumptuary laws which regulated every facet of a person's life, down to the type of clothes he could wear, the breed of horse he could ride, and the type of hawk he could fly.

"You're well mounted, friar," Falcon said pointedly. He noted that the man's feet were covered by shoes of fine Cordoba leather, sewn with tiny seed pearls. Barefoot friars indeed! Falcon thought.

"I ride on the Holy Father's business," Benedetto said.

"For this reason, I am spared the customary asceticism of my order. It is a long walk from Rome to Paris."

"Since when have Franciscan friars been acting as papal legates?" Falcon asked. The Franciscans, once the most devoted of ministers to the poor, had grown uncommonly lax of late.

"The Holy Father finds my particular skills of some use," Benedetto answered. "As a mendicant friar, I am under the authority of no abbot and thus I report only to the Throne of St. Peter. I am of sufficiently high birth to speak in the highest courts of Christendom, and I speak a number of languages. Let us say that, if not indispensable, I am at least not without value."

"For how much longer, I wonder?" Gudrun said. Falcon could not help smiling at the look of sour discomfit that crossed the friar's face. The new Pope was Innocent III, and for the first time in generations a genuinely good, religious and capable man wore the Fisherman's ring. He was engaged in a thorough housecleaning in Rome, and was purging the higher clergy of its worst elements. He was doing much to restore the tattered prestige of the papacy, but his influence was still unfelt here in France, and probably would not be for years.

"My lady," Benedetto began, "I am quite—" His words were cut short by the appearance of a band of men on the road before them. There were at least twenty of them, and Falcon didn't like their look. Six were mounted, the rest on foot. The footmen were common outlaws. Most had lopped ears, branded foreheads, or lumps of scar where their noses had been: the marks of the public executioner. The mounted men wore helmets and rusty armor, but their spurs were of plain steel, the sign of men who had been degraded from the status of knighthood.

"Stand where you are!" shouted one. "We want your goods and no more. Lay down your arms and pile everything you have in the road, then you can go freely." The bandits were eying Gudrun greedily.

"They're lying," Falcon said. "They'll take any who can be held for ransom prisoner and kill the rest."

"You must save us," Benedetto said.

"How?" retorted Gudrun.

Wulf rode up to Falcon and tossed him a twenty-foot lance with an ash shaft. The younger man readied his own weapons: a short curved sword and a small round shield. He studied the men before them.

"Too many, my lord," he said. "Too many even for you."

"I don't like bandits," Falcon said, glaring at the men.

"Who does? They are still too many. Let's get away from here while we can."

"You would not leave us?" Gudrun protested.

"The lady can come with us," Wulf said. "Her horse is a good one and she rides well. What use have we for a pack of townsmen? Let's go!"

Falcon never took his glare off the bandits. With a snarl he trotted his mount forward. Wulf sighed and followed his master. Falcon stopped about ten yards in front of the bandits.

"This group includes pilgrims and churchmen," Falcon said. "You risk excommunication." The bandits merely laughed.

"Do you think we fear that?" said one. Falcon had not expected them to.

He was too close to charge, and all the men held their shields low. Without warning, he raised the lance and cast it like a javelin at one of the horsemen. Taken completely by surprise, the man toppled from his horse with the ash pole through his throat.

With a roar, Falcon spurred his horse into the midst of his disconcerted foes. He tore his ax from its place and brought it down on a helmet with an audible crunch. Wulf sprang from his saddle and dashed to his master's left side. From this position, he repelled any of the footmen who tried to attack Falcon from his left rear, always a horseman's most vulnerable spot against foot attack.

The bandits were disconcerted for a moment at the fury of the attack, but they quickly regained the initiative and encircled the two men, the horsemen keeping them at lancepoint while the footmen rushed in for the kill like wolves.

"Break out, Draco!" Wulf shouted. "We can't beat them like this!"

"Mount behind me!" Falcon ordered. He knew that it was useless. The instant Wulf turned his back, he'd get an ax in it and even his excellent mail wouldn't save him.

Then there was a thunder of hooves and three horsemen were breaking through the circle of bandits, hewing right and left with their long swords. Falcon shouted with joyous rage at this unexpected aid, and then he was spurring back among the outlaws, his long, curved sword now out, flickering in bewildering arcs and dealing pain or death at every cut. Within seconds, the remnants of the bandits were fleeing into the woods, where the trees grew too thick for mounted pursuit. Falcon chased them as far as the edge of the wood, then turned back to thank his rescuers. Wulf ran up to him, holding out a piece of cloth cut from one of the bandits' tunics. As Falcon cleaned his blade, Wulf said in a low voice: "Look who we've fallen in with, my lord."

Falcon cantered over to the three knights. All wore excellent armor and face-covering helmets, which they were removing. All were dressed in identical white surcoats over their armor. The surcoats bore a red cross. Their shields were likewise white with red crosses. "Templars, by God!" Falcon whispered. He had good reason to distrust the Knights of the Temple. He had seen the last of the old order cut down defending the Beauséant, famed standard of the Templars, at the disastrous battle of Hattin. The order had been rebuilt by Gerard de Ridemont, grand master of the Templars, and Falcon knew them to be something far more sinister than the crusading order they had been for so long. Still, these men had saved his life, and he had to put the best face on it. He cantered over to them.

"I am Sir Draco Falcon, and I thank you for your aid, good sirs."

One of the men threw back his coif to reveal sandy hair and blue eyes. He was very young, no more than about twenty-two. "I am Claude de Coucy," he said. "My brothers and I were on our way to the Temple outside Paris when some local people told us of these bandits and we rode looking for them. We are pleased to have found you in time to be of assistance." In spite of his distrust, Falcon found himself liking the young knight. The other two were older men who spoke little except curtly to acknowledge Falcon's thanks.

Gudrun and the other travelers came up, loud in their praise of Falcon and the Templars. "It was like some old hero tale," Gudrun exclaimed. "First Sir Draco taking on all those men by himself, then these gentlemen appearing just when all seemed lost." Wulf looked annoyed when his own part in the affray was slighted, but life had accustomed him to the insensitivity of his betters. "Will you ride with us to Paris?"

"We should be honored, lady," Sir Claude said, taking her hand and kissing it. The warrior-monks were supposed to be bound by a vow of chastity, but this one hadn't forgotten his courtly manners.

"With such men as you four riding with us," Gudrun said, "we need fear nothing." Falcon wanted nothing to do with Templars, but now there was nothing he could do about it. His jaw set in a grim line, he rode beside the white-robed men down the road to Paris, brooding on the devious minds of women, friars, and crusading knights.

About the Author

MARK RAMSAY was born on St. John's Day, 1947. He is a professional writer and he lives on a remote mountaintop in the Appalachian Mountains. When not writing, he pursues his lifelong study of the Medieval and Classical periods. He makes his own weapons and armor and sometimes fights with them, when he can find someone to practice with. He feels this brings a breath of authenticity to his writing.